The Corsican Trap

Books by Linda Mann

The Tavistock Allan Mystery Series
Mist
The Tidemaster
The Corsican Trap

The Mr Boots Series
Mr Boots

To Emma, Henry and Lucy with love

Although this book is set in and around the Isle of Man and there really is a theatre called The Gaiety Theatre and it does have more than a few ghosts, all other characters and some of the locations are purely fictitious and any similarity to anybody living or indeed dead is simply coincidence and the product of my overworked imagination and far too many dried frog pills.

The Corsican Trap

LINDA MANN

Acknowledgements

With many thanks to Mervin Stokes for kindly reading the finished manuscript and for ensuring that the technical bits were corrected without my having to change the plot, such as it is.

To Dave Bell and other members of the Isle of Man constabulary for escorting me around police headquarters and for not asking too many awkward questions over my sudden interest in concrete.

To Frances Hackeson for the calm and professional production of another book and for all her help over the author queries.

To Victoria Harrop for her unfailing patience and expertise over the front cover and for doing gothic for me.

To Ruth Baxendale, Kay Austin and Kevin Walker-Smith for reading through yet another insult to literature and for laughing at the bits which were actually deliberately funny.

To Gillian Hush for giving me my annual boost in the ego and metaphoric kick-start …

To my children who have come to terms with having a

MAD mother and their father who admitted that the old writing had improved a bit …

And lastly to Messrs Gordon of London who make a very good gin!

Prologue

The Isle of Man is a solitary piece of often damp rock, thirty-two-and-a-half miles long and thirteen-and-a-half miles wide, squatting morosely in the middle of the Irish Sea roughly central to Scotland, Ireland, Wales and England.

Various storytellers would have us believe that the Island was originally land torn from the coast of Northern Island and tossed into the Irish Sea by an irate drunken giant, who had lost a game of cards or possibly dice. However, other less imaginative and more prosaic souls, commonly referred to as geologists, hold firmly to the idea that it was originally formed by a ridge of volcanoes.

Whatever the Island's history, it stands today proud of its heritage, its Parliament (the oldest in the world) and its people, even the very small ones who live under the fairy bridge and allegedly pinch your hub caps and disable your engine if you don't say 'Hello'.

The Island also has a few theatres, the oldest and by far the prettiest being the Gaiety Theatre. This hive of entertainment is prominently situated on the Harris Promenade in Douglas, gleaming in its new shiny paint and polished brass, a bastion of all that is and was Victorian. Rebuilt by the renowned architect Frank Matcham at the turn of the century and saved by the Isle of Man Government and an act of Tynwald in the 1970s, it survives today as a proud reminder of the Island's tourist heyday.

It also harbours a small coterie of ghosts.

* * *

The Gaiety Theatre sat facing the rising tide and waited for the next production. Lights had been switched off, seats had been cleared and the detritus left by a previous audience had been removed by an aged and grumpy cleaner accompanied by a spotty youth on work experience.

Somewhere in the backyard gloom of the stage a carpenter hammered to the accompaniment of the latest thing in half-clad and nubile girl bands, which was being loudly plugged to death on one of the local radio stations. Above him, dust motes shuffled downwards, at first caught by the glow of a bare bulb and then studiously ignored as they settled on the ropes and canvas looped around the partially painted and temporarily waiting set, which contained a pair of elderly French windows, an ancient faded red velvet suite and a writing desk riddled with asthmatic woodworm.

High above the stalls and the corridor that led from the stage to the audience, a long room habitually used for the storing of props and ancient paint, echoed to the sound of voices raised in argument and barely concealed dislike. The voices belonged to four figures ornately dressed as if for a three-act costume drama by George Bernard Shaw or Oscar Wilde. They were all seated around a wooden table and were staring intently at a small, garishly printed flyer. There was a brief silence followed by a collective and heartfelt groan.

"Oh Gods, not another bloody amateur debacle," a large, distinguished looking gentleman sporting a luxuriant handlebar moustache with matching side whiskers, a spotless purple silk cravat and a dark blue velvet smoking jacket loudly declared. The only lady in the group patted her strawberry blonde curled locks, and adjusting the camellia at her bosom for maximum effect, leant across the expanse of darkened oak and purred with agreement, "Darling Edwin, so very right, as usual."

"Gloria my angel, I knew that you, of all people, would understand." Edwin, the owner of the overly cultivated facial hair reached across the table and stroked her hand, whilst staring lovingly down the front of her gently undulating and magnificently filled bodice.

"Forgive me while I leave the room to vomit," the third man muttered. Turning away from the fond couple in as pointed a fashion as he could, he fixed his thin, ascetic features upon the middle-aged gentleman seated at the far end of the table in a steely frown. "Well Rupert, what do you think?" he asked.

The fourth gentleman sat thoughtfully stroking his goatee beard, which sprouted in a thin point from his chin, until he could plainly see that he had all the other occupants' collective and undivided attention. Ponderously he stood up, tossing his coat tails behind him with a practised hand.

"Gentlemen, and you of course dear lady, I really feel – quite strongly in fact – that as the amateurs have actually kept this place above water for some considerable time we ought to just leave them to get on with it."

"But have you actually seen what they intend to sabotage?" Edwin shouted.

"'Blithe Spirit'."

"A masterpiece, an absolute and utter gem of a play. I remember how I wowed the audience with my talk of nasturtiums and as for the final denouement … I was magnificent, superb …"

"I'm sure you were excellent, my dear Edwin, as the arrogant and much fêted writer, but that really isn't a good enough reason to ruin it for the current cast," the third man muttered.

"Now look hear, Cedric old fruit, I really don't see why not …"

"Because the last thing we actually need at the moment is for Russell to have a few well chosen words with the new Theatre Chaplain," Rupert advised him in well modulated and carefully articulated vowels, each consonant placed for maximum effect.

"Please tell me he's not another whey-faced fundamentalist with a crucifixion fixation?"

"Unfortunately not. He is actually a she …"

"A woman priest!"

"Vicar, Edwin, they call them Vicars."

"Whatever next, some bosky Brunhilde running the Island?"

There was a brief hiatus broken by a ballerina in a skimpy white tutu pirouetting through the wall and back again.

"I really do wish that they wouldn't do that," Gloria complained, her heavily carmined mouth taking on a petulant twist.

"Brainless ninnies," Edwin declared.

"Low blood sugar," Rupert barked, screwing up the playbill and dropping it on the floor. "All that dieting," he explained on seeing Gloria's blank expression.

"Oh."

"Anyway if it wasn't next week's dismembering of Noel Coward that you wanted to discuss with us Rupert old chap, what did you call us in for?" Cedric asked, sitting back down at the table and tipping his chair up onto two shabby legs.

Rupert took a deep theatrical breath and gave a small well crafted shudder before replying. "My dears, I have just returned from the Manager's office, where I have discovered that the department of Tourism and Tasteless Entertainments have come up with another of their money making debacles."

"Oh yes?" Cedric enquired, leaning forward and tipping the chair back onto all four stumps.

"The powers that be, including the Hairy Helmet and the Collective Council of Piffle Spouters, have decided to allow that ghastly reality ghost-hunter and his assembled crew to stay overnight in the theatre for some midsummer special."

"Good grief! You can't mean … Not the ginger-haired idiot, the one that always sees hooded figures dragging bodies around by their feet?" Cedric barked. "Threw a perfectly decent double gin and slim at him once, missed the telly completely, landed in poor old Russell's lap."

"Ah."

"Brand new pair of trousers, and the ice in the crotch didn't go down well I can tell you."

"Ah. Was he entertaining?" Edwin enquired with a grin.

"As luck would have it, no."

"And they are actually going to allow that … that awful little man to stay the night?" Gloria swallowed hard and looked uneasily around.

"Apparently so, together with the diminutive blonde and a cast of thousands … plus a large Alsatian called Mike."

"Damn."

"Language Edwin, language. Ladies present and all that," Rupert growled.

"Ladies?" Cedric enquired, an evil glint in his eye. Gloria glared at him and readjusted her cleavage.

"Mad Harry will go …"

"Mad?" Rupert prompted unsmilingly.

"Yes."

They sat in pensive silence, broken intermittently by the faint clicking of a death-watch beetle, which was methodically nibbling its slow way to freedom in one of the wooden beams below their feet.

They all knew, without being told, that the black lady who sat in the stalls could be bribed with a night haunting the honeymoon suite at the Sefton Hotel next door. Even the dancers could, at a pinch, be persuaded not to scurry across the now non-existent gallery between the old and the newer parts of the theatre, but old Harry was just mad. Rupert eyed his colleagues speculatively and finally voiced their collective worry.

"It's the combination of the two that concerns me most, my dears. There is of course that scene with the seance, and whoever the Middling Players have chosen as Madame Arcati is bound to get at least part of it right and Harry always objects when they start moving the glass around."

"You mean?"

"Unfortunately, as soon as Harry spots the board and the follicly challenged tit pontificating into camera he will take immediate and instant umbrage, calculated to improve ratings enormously and to ring the death knell over any peace and quiet we may have been lucky enough to have retained here for the last fifty or so years."

"Then what in heavens name are we to do?" Cedric groaned despairingly.

"We have a tenants meeting and, if the others agree, we go straight down to Russell and get him to do something."

Rupert looked desperately around. Russell Gillings-Cooper may not have been his idea of the perfect Theatre Manager but at that moment he was the only one they had, and like all other Managers before him had finally managed to achieve a workable truce with the theatre ghosts and other assorted entities, including a shy and diffident poltergeist called Mervin who lurked in the boiler room and had an almost pathological dislike of actors. The only Manager not to have achieved this state of affairs had been pushed unceremoniously from the upper circle by Mad Harry himself and the blood and other sticky bits had taken several hours of hard scrubbing to get off the seat covers in the stalls.

"Perhaps he won't take it that badly, if we ask him nicely?" Gloria announced hopefully.

"My dear young lady, you may indeed have taken the royal box by storm during your West End debut but even your many and obvious charms will not impress the big man downstairs. No, I'm afraid that we are all going to be in for a rough and rocky ride and if there isn't blood on the carpet and ectoplasm on the walls by the end of today, well I'll be a Dutchman." And on that parting shot, Rupert picked up his polished Malacca cane and a darkly gleaming top hat and vanished with a bow.

"I know I shouldn't fuss darling, but I have a horrible

premonition of impending doom and you know, sweetie, that I'm hardly ever wrong," Gloria sniffed piteously, whilst at the same time delicately wiping a glint of wetness from the corner of a heavily painted eye with her index finger.

"Now, now, my little honey bunny, none of that or you'll look like a panda all the way through the matinée performance," Edwin declared, handing her a grey-looking square of linen. Gloria gulped and then blew her nose so loudly that three sharp featured ballerinas poked their heads through the adjoining wall.

"Is Harry really going to, you know ..." Her voice tailed weakly away and the dancers looked from one to the other with avid and silent interest.

"Put it this way, if that psychic shyster actually has the temerity to visit the traps in the basement, Harry will tear an appendage off and beat him to death with the wet end," Cedric muttered in accents of undisguised relish.

"Oh, that bad."

"Yes, Gloria my little artichoke, it will indeed be that bad," Edwin agreed, before kicking Cedric in the shins and fixing him with a look of intense dislike bordering on hatred. Cedric glared back at him and stuck his tongue out in a childish display of antagonism and vanished. Gloria rose from her chair and fluttered over to where her lover was still sitting and kissed him on his puckered forehead.

"I'm sure it won't actually be that bad," she cooed, "after all, Rupert will have a word with him and it will all calm down and be fine." Edwin, still thoroughly unconvinced, nodded his head in agreement and then taking his beloved Gloria in his arms, slowly merged with the surrounding air and they both faded gently into the prevailing gloom.

The three dancers who had been eavesdropping from

behind the wall looked at each other with identical painted faces of consternation and then muttered as one, "We'd better tell Madame," before they too floated silently backwards.

* * *

Russell Gillings-Cooper closed the heavy theatre doors and leaning back against the glass panelled surface uttered a heartfelt sigh. He alone knew with a sinking heart that what his masters were about to do was quite possibly the daftest thing some demented administrator with a Himmler fixation and the brainpower of a sponge had ever previously perpetrated. He could, he thought, take a long holiday somewhere hot and without a current extradition treaty or he could plead sickness on the ground of Post Traumatic Stress Disorder and retire to his bijou apartment on the promenade.

Rupert suddenly appeared before his tired eyes and prodded him in the stomach with the silver top of his cane.

"Ah," Russell muttered, "You've heard?"

"Yes, and the question we are all dying to have answered is the one demanding to know what you are going to do about it?"

"Rupert my old friend, I have absolutely no bloody idea at all."

* * *

Deep in a dank, dark cellar, the firm of Brew & Kermode, builders of distinction and known by everyone in the trade as 'The Flintstones' were having the usual problems with the brief given to them earlier by their employer's architect. Fred Brew looked down at the metal sheet under his feet and pushing his safety helmet to one side, scratched the hairy lobe of a dust-encrusted ear. "Bugger," he swore and then spat on the floor.

His companion Barnabas (Barney) Kermode, a middle-aged and portly individual with a spade and a large expanse of builder's cleavage, sighed and muttered "Oh aye. Well …"

"Thing is …"

"Aye …"

"This isn't supposed to be here."

"That's what they said, aye."

"Bit of concrete, they said. Underneath the old lino is what they said, not a ruddy great sheet of old tin …"

"Well now …"

"Take the lino up and renew the old concrete so's they can lower the level of the floor and stick in a bar, that's what they said."

"Good idea that …"

"What is?"

"Having a bar down here, convivial that. Do you remember old Clary Corlett?"

"Him that lived out at Port Soderick?"

"No not him, the other one."

"The one that married Mona Creer as was."

"Aye."

"Knockers the size of melons and I'm not talking about the little yellow ones neither." Fred grinned broadly and leant against his pick. "He had a bar in a cellar, cosy it were and warm until that pipe burst."

"Aye, shame."

"Still what are we going to do with this? It's all stuck down on the old mix, be a devil to get off and me pick won't go through it."

"Hmm …"

"Well …?"

"I reckon we dig around it with that there pick, then prize it off with a crowbar, or a hammer and chisel – you never know, luck and the fairies might be with us and the bugger might just come off easy."

"That's what I was thinking, mind you this is going to cost somebody extra, this is."

There was a gentle mutter of disapproval as Fred hefted his pickaxe and Barney wielded his spade to clear the debris. After a short while they both stopped, and wiping sweat from their respective brows, regarded the solitary sheet of old metal, now heavily dented, with a jaundiced and experienced air.

"This," Barney declared, leaning heavily upon his digging implement, "is going to take all day."

"Aye well, it will that, and then some." Fred agreed resting his grime-encrusted pickaxe against the cellar wall. "Fancy a brew and a bap?" he asked.

"Well, now then, I wouldn't say no. It's thirsty work this and no mistake," Barney replied.

Some time later they sat on a collection of upturned wooden pallets and drums and drank ebony-coloured tea to the accompaniment of a Manx Radio broadcaster who was trying to fascinate the general public with his visit to a local concrete factory.

"Bet they do better stuff 'n this," Barney observed, poking a portion of concrete, which now coyly peaked from under the mutilated tin, with his foot.

"Must be English," Fred agreed, poking in the dust with the end of a wooden dowel.

Something glinted in the surface of the exposed floor

and winked silver in the glare of the solitary naked light bulb. The bulb hung forlornly from a length of grubby wire suspended from the ceiling and swung erratically every time Fred wielded his tool of choice, thereby creating weird shadows on the dusty pockmarked walls.

"What's this?" Fred asked, and bent down to take a closer look.

The glinting silver appeared to be a watch strap firmly embedded in the concrete under a corner of the obstinate metal barrier. Quickly grabbing a hammer and chisel, Fred proceeded to carefully shatter the cement mix surrounding the expensive looking object.

"Blow me but I reckon this could be a Rolex." Fred remarked in cheerful tones as he bent to his task.

"What bugger would be daft enough to drop something like that in wet cement? You'd fish it out before it set," Barney reasoned, as he bit enthusiastically into his still warm bacon bap. A dribble of brown sauce dropped to the floor.

Fred Brew applied the chisel with renewed enthusiasm laced with greed, and the concrete beneath his gaze shattered, releasing its grip on the watch and the wrist bone to which it had been attached.

Fred swore and backed off, clutching his tools in both hands, a look of horror on his features.

Barney, who had observed the finding of the skeletal hand, grinned.

"Suppose you want me to call the police now, don't you?" he asked, laying down his cup and remaining crust on a flattened brown paper bag.

"Suppose we'll have to," Fred reluctantly agreed.

"Mind you, this will put everything back a bit, won't

it?" he observed. "I mean, by the time they get down here and dig the rest of it up, it could be days before we get this finished. Weeks even."

"And we get paid by the hour," Barney rumbled, as he finally found his mobile phone in one of his many and commodious pockets.

"Bit of luck that then," he agreed punching the numbers.

"Police?" he enquired, upon being connected to a cheery soul. "We think we may have found a body you might like to see …" Barney listened and then gave a deep melodious chuckle. "No there's no urgency, officer, 'cos I really don't think this one's going anywhere, although you may need a selection of industrial power tools to retrieve it."

An hour later Detective Inspector Brian Clague surveyed the skeletal remains with a practised eye. It was definitely a hand and it was still attached to what he hoped would be the rest of the body. Fred and Barney hovered in a corner looking quite pleased about the break in routine. Brian moved unhurriedly towards them as the sniffer dog arrived.

"So which one of you found the deceased?" Brian asked.

"I did," Fred replied.

"And the bones were under the tin?"

"Tin sheet – you mix the concrete up on a sheet and then you spade it in the hole see, whoever buried it must have wanted to cover it up see …"

"'Cos it would float," Barney interjected with enthusiasm. "Get stuff fall into the mix, long tails and such, they float to the top, mess the surface up something rotten. If you don't want to have to re-lay it you have to pierce then in the guts with something sharp and then push 'em down. Not that I have, mind," he added in a hasty fashion as Fred gave him a deeply suspicious look.

"Wouldn't be at all professional leaving bodies in the mix, causes a void in the slab, and you couldn't stick something heavy on top 'cos it would collapse inwards … eventually," Fred observed, rolling himself a cigarette.

"Well if it was a big something, say a cat or a very large long tail," Barney added before spitting on the ground. He had almost said the word 'rat' out loud which everyone knew was traditionally one of the unluckiest words to use, and in front of a policeman. 'And,' he thought, 'it's not as if we don't have enough bad luck already what with bodies, substandard concrete and a distinct lack of the correct brand of brown sauce in the mid-morning bap.'

"Right," Brian muttered, watching the dog sniffing eagerly around the metal square.

"Can't be that far down anyways," Fred remarked, licking the end of a Rizla paper.

"Oh, why?"

"Well, the stuff under the sheet was coming away too easy, all flaky and such."

"Right."

"Poor bugger," Barney observed. "Wonder how he died?"

"He?"

"Well I suppose it could be a she. Not natural anyway, you don't roll a tin sheet over someone then stick down a load of lino and finally brick it all in 'cos someone died of natural causes, do you?" Barney snorted.

"This was bricked up?" Brian asked, making a mental note to find the current and previous owners as soon as possible.

"Oh aye, no one knew this place had a cellar, until some tit went through the floor above and found this place, then we went round until they found the cellar door plastered over by the side of the stairs and knocked through. Next thing we know the new owners had a quick look-see and reckoned it was a great space for a bar, no windows, walled sides, concealed lighting and a few upturned beer barrels and Bob's your Uncle."

"God, I wish he was and that he was here," Brian thought.

The dog suddenly started barking and then with hackles raised and a look of madness in its eyes, backed away towards the door, growling.

The hairs on the nape of Brian's neck stood up.

Fred and Barney watched with total unconcern as the dog was removed by his handler, growling, snarling and slobbering.

"So what was all that about?" Barney asked.

"Dunno, might have something to do with the sudden drop in temperature," Fred rumbled, finally getting the soggy roll-up to glow red at the end furthest away from his mouth.

"You know what them Resurrectionists believed?"

"Who?"

"People long time ago."

"Oh, them."

"They believed that unless you had a body your soul couldn't go to heaven, that's why they wouldn't leave their bodies to science like what we would."

"I remember now, people used to go down the graveyard, dig the newly buried bodies up and sell them to the doctors for summat or other, saw something on one of them history channels. Put me off me egg 'n chips it did."

"Aye well perhaps now that we've found him or her, he or she is back?"

"What – you mean like a ghost like?"

"Oh aye."

"And the dog ..."

"They say animals can see ghosts."

"Oh, right."

Brian, who had up to that point been listening to both pontificating builders with increasing amusement as he measured up the area still covered by the metal sheet, turned and stared at them.

"Not that I believe in them mind, ghosts that is, only it was nice and warm before you lot turned up," Barney observed, picking up his bag of tools from where he'd left them.

"So can we go now?" Fred asked.

"What, oh yes, just leave a number where we can contact you," Brian replied almost absentmindedly.

Fred and Barney removed themselves and their personal effects in a matter of seconds and Brian was left standing under the naked bulb in a cold damp cellar with the distinct feeling, that although technically he was the only living person remaining, he was definitely not alone.

* * *

Mannanan Mac Lir, minor deity, third-class, failed, looked at the vast expanse of calm flat water in a tasteful shade of blue and scowled horribly. Valhalla, Nirvana or Heaven, depending on your religious preference, was absolutely perfect. The sea was always blue, the sun always shone and the gardens, magnificent in their floral displays of horticultural one-upmanship, were simply the best you could ever get, anywhere. 'And,' Mannanan thought miserably, 'not a coloured ball on a stick in sight.'

The women were built in the time-honoured tradition beloved by painters down the ages and wore very little clothing, as if to emphasise the fact that big was definitely beautiful and they came in any colour you liked, including oddly enough, green. But …

Mannanan miserably stared across the sea and flicked a small flat pebble onto the ripple-free surface; it bounced and then it bounced some more. Mannanan watched incredulously as it bounced out of sight. Some time later he heard a faint cry followed by an irate voice demanding to know who had thrown it.

He was on the verge of leaving when a large, well oiled, pink and rumpled body plonked itself down on the ground next to him and handed him a brimming horn of what was officially called nectar and what Mannanan privately thought of as mead and not particularly good mead at that. "Brought you a little drinkie," his sweating companion stated, wiping a bead of perspiration from his brow with the corner of his gold-edged toga.

"Humph," Mannanan growled.

"So how did the meeting go?" his companion asked, mid-slurp.

"I have been downgraded to that of the average spook with poltergeist tendencies."

"Ah. Bit brutal that."

"They said that I had exceeded my original brief and that I'd brought the whole God business into disrepute."

"And what did you say?"

"Nothing."

"Nothing!"

"Oh come on, Bacchus old chap, what could I say?"

"Well …"

"They were absolutely right. After all, if I'd done something in the first place and actually admitted that I'd made a mistake that last time, people wouldn't have died and that wretched writer would even now be roaming freely and not doped up to the eyeballs in some holding pen for the criminally insane. Pride, Bacchus old pal, is not a good thing to have if you're over a thousand years dead and set in your ways."

"No I suppose not, mind you it's why most of us are here."

"True." Mannanan took a gulp of mead and relaxed a fraction.

"You know what I really hate?"

"No, what?"

"I hate the fact that it's so perfect, nothing is out of place, no grain of sand is the wrong shade of white, no ripple more than the standard 3.2 mm and everybody smiles. It's like some dammed politically correct holiday destination of peace and relaxation."

"Ah."

"Mind you, it wasn't as if I didn't enjoy it all at first; I did, but like most holidays if it's more than two weeks you start wondering if you'd turned everything off before you left, and whether the plants need watering."

"You don't have things to turn off, you have the Isle of Man … mind you I suppose in a way …" Bacchus mused, as several ideas hit his addled brain at the same time.

"And I'd like to play a round of golf in the rain with a twenty-knot wind and not a vestige of a chance of getting to the nineteenth hole before the sky falls on your head."

"Oh, you mean you're bored."

"You have no idea."

"But this place was designed to please."

"It did in the beginning, it really did, but now I'd do almost anything to watch a couple of decent sized brackish waves and get nicely wet and miserable, even that infernal wretched mist would make a nice change from all of this."

"Some people are never happy."

"I guess once a miserable git ..."

"Always a miserable git."

"Afraid so."

Bacchus watched his old friend and with a sigh stood up. "I shall, I believe, really miss you," he stated, tipping the last of his drink onto the sand.

"What?" Mannanan asked, looking up at him in a puzzled fashion.

"You're going home."

"Home?"

"The Isle of Man."

"Bacchus old pal, just exactly how much of this dreadful stuff have you drunk?"

"Not enough." Bacchus sighed again and pointed out to sea. A small dark blob appeared over the distant horizon, growing larger and blacker as it got nearer.

"But how? I mean why? ..."

"We had a meeting, sort of and decided that all things considered and trust me when I say that we considered most of them, that the best thing to do with you was to send you back, minus your special status."

"But I still don't see why?"

"You know how you can go to some really good party and there's always some miserable old sod who's given up smoking, won't drink, won't dance and has taken a vow of chastity."

"Er ..."

"You are, I'm afraid, the weakest link, and frankly old fruit, if allowed to stay much longer in serious danger of ruining it for the rest of us."

"Oh, sorry."

"Don't be, it's probably the Scots in you."

"So I'm going back."

"As soon as you've packed, we did think of having a party but in the circumstances ..."

"Right, I'll just throw a few things in a bag."

"You can take Claws if you want."

"Really?"

"She's all yours. Majority decision, unanimous really."

Mannanan smiled, in fact for once in his life he actually beamed. He was going home.

Back to a place of rain-washed glowering cliffs and a permanently lazy wind which never bothered about whistling around its shivering victims but went straight through them. He would be back to stalking amongst the heather and anarchic sheep up on the mountains, fog-shrouded and evilly damp.

Some time later he stood on a sun-drenched golden beach, watching small children jumping into the sea, surrounded on all sides by happy holidaymakers and even happier concession owners. Claws, a large, chocolate-brown, long-haired Manx cat, looked up at him with brilliant turquoise eyes and mewled. Mannanan bent down to stroke her shaggy head and with a note of apology in his voice, assured her that they were definitely home, even if it didn't much resemble the place they had once lived.

There was a sudden roar of sound, a flurry of whistles and cat calls and a large Honda motorbike roared past them, the rider completely naked, apart from a pair of boots with white socks and the obligatory crash helmet.

"On the other hand I could be wrong," Mannanan grinned, picking up his bag in one hand and the cat in the other. "Let's just go see if anyone we know is in."

Chapter One

A short stocky man, on the shady side of middle age with the facial jowls of a particularly wrinkled and sorrowful bloodhound, stood outside the aged façade of the Benedict Hotel in Douglas and avidly watched the removal of several skiploads of builder's rubbish. His interest, however, like the other sightseers clustered around a makeshift barrier loosely decorated with blue and white police tape, was mostly concentrated upon something long and heavy and covered from stem to stern with thick black plastic sheeting, which was being unhurriedly removed by several bowed figures wearing fluorescent yellow jackets.

He stuck his hands deep in the tartan-lined innards of his Burberry trench coat and fiddled with the keys in his pocket.

A burly youth detached himself from the mêlée of police and workmen and sauntered over to stand beside him. "Got a cigarette, mate?" he asked, and then, after extracting one from a packet of Marlboro, leant towards the watcher, his hands cupped around a freely proffered light and whispered. "They think it's a male, Mr West, been there about thirty or possibly forty years – no idea as yet as to the identity."

"Thanks Daryl, the cash will be in the post, usual method."

"Anything else I can do for you Mr West, you just let me know eh?" Daryl touched his index finger to his nose and with a sly grin sauntered off towards a grimy white van.

The man took a deep breath of seaweed-laden air and turned back towards the front of Douglas promenade. Old tenements and guesthouses jostled each other in various shades of white and grey, windows masked with heavy lengths of net and pink ruffled curtains. Hanging baskets filled to the brim with petunias and multi-coloured lobelia danced in the freshening wind and were totally disregarded by the solitary walker.

He stopped when he reached the promenade and then barely noticing the approaching traffic, including a large horse called Ned who was nonchalantly pulling a tram, strode across the road to a vacant bench.

He sat and stared at the few tourists braving the chill of the Irish Sea as if mesmerised by their foolhardy bravery.

'Well,' he thought, 'it was bound to happen sometime and basically I've been damned lucky that it hasn't happened before'. He tried vainly to remember if he had left anything behind, but it had been such a long time ago. The mobile telephone in his pocket blithely chirruped and he extracted it with something akin to reluctance.

"Yes," he barked, "West speaking."

He listened and then smiled.

"Of course I would be delighted to sponsor such a play ... But Laura, you know that I've always liked Noel Coward, all that froth and wit … the who? … Ah, I see your point … still the minister must be used to the vagaries of the amateur mind … after all he's been attending meetings of Tynwald for as long as I've been running this damn company … speaking of which I'd like you to get my broker on the line … I can wait … just patch him through …" West sat, the sun beating down on his balding head and little beads of perspiration trickling down the nape of his neck. Finally another voice growled from the confines of the plastic ovoid he still held in one tanned and wrinkled hand.

"Ah, Arthur old chap, just a quick word, I'm thinking of going fishing full time … Yes I know … but the thing is that I have just had a good offer from one of the big boys for the firm as it stands … shouldn't think I could do better so I've decided to go for an earlier retirement than we'd originally planned … Yes just liquidate all that you can and put the property on the market … Chelsea doesn't have to sign or know a thing and neither do the other wives … because I've settled enough on them over the years and I'm not doing it again especially if I don't legally need to … exactly … No don't call me, I'll give you a bell next week, and Arthur, do it ever so quietly and there'll be a nice fat bonus in the post just for you." He flipped the cover back down and then secreted it in one of his many pockets.

The Isle of Man was changing, regulatory paperwork that used to be routinely avoided or ignored was now forwarded to him with Gestapo-like efficiency and the penalties for non-completion would have received a standing ovation from any senior official of the old guard politburo. The old boy network of elder statesmen and their respective 'Sir Humphreys' that he'd relied on for years was also dying out and in some cases quite literally. He'd had to attend three funerals the previous week and none of them had been as old as him.

"I dunno," he mused, almost smiling, "you take up jogging, eat low fat, high fibre rabbit food, abstain from nicotine, alcohol and red meat and what happens? I'll tell you what happens – some bugger in a souped-up Ford Escort with no brakes, insurance or a valid licence loses it on the bend and ploughs into the side of your oncoming Jaguar, that's what happens! Either that or you drop down dead doing warm-up laps."

He smiled at the vicious irony of it all and stood up. "And I will take it with me, all the way to somewhere hot and sultry; tax-free and totally devoid of any bloodsucking relatives past or for that matter present," he chortled softly.

⋆ ⋆ ⋆

Tavistock Allan, writer, mother and general factotum glared at the heap of damp and soggy material on the utility room floor and muttered a string of very rude words. There were at least two more loads of smelly washing in front of her and she would have sworn on a stack of bibles that they hadn't been there earlier on.

So much for reading the galley proofs of her latest insult to good literature. She looked around at the mess created by three children, their friends and a weekend husband, sighed very loudly, turned and stomped back to the kitchen to switch the kettle on.

She'd just pushed the plunger on the cafetière, opened up a packet of chocolate digestives and turned on the television, when the doorbell boomed electronically from the hall.

She gritted her teeth, set the cafetière back on its cork

mat and stalked down the ill-lit hallway.

Tavistock opened the front door and glared at her unexpected visitor. Bob Callow stood on the doorstep and grinned back at her.

"Ah, coffee," he muttered appreciatively as he sniffed the air now redolent with the aroma of freshly ground fairtrade Columbian coffee beans. Tavistock glowered back at him and then as he obviously had no intention of going, reluctantly gestured for him to come in. Bob smiled and walked straight past her into the lounge.

"Bob …"

"You don't actually watch that rubbish, do you?" he asked, pointing to the flickering television screen.

"Yes, not that it's …"

"So what's our Lorraine up to today?" he enquired, moving a magazine and a plastic weapon of mass destruction from one of the armchairs to a space on the floor before sitting down, a stealthily acquired chocolate biscuit clutched in his hand.

"Interviewing an ageing rock star and unleashing the latest in uplift water bras on an unsuspecting public," Tavistock grumpily answered as she padded back to the kitchen for another cup and the milk.

When she returned Bob was on his second biscuit, and having already poured himself a coffee from the waiting pot into her waiting cup, gaily slurping. Tavistock gave him a decidedly dirty look and handed him the opened milk carton.

"And to what do I owe this dubious visit?" she snarled, grabbing the cafetière in one hand and the television remote in the other.

"Oi," Bob exclaimed as the screen suddenly went black,

"I was watching that!"

"What could you possibly find interesting in a couple of scantily clad women parading about in frilly underwear?"

"Well …"

"Grow up, get a life, preferably not mine and tell me why you're here and not at work making the streets safe for the great Manx public."

"I've quit."

There was a short stunned silence and then Tavistock handed back the biscuits.

"Why?"

"Well, all right, I haven't actually resigned as such."

"Good."

"I've taken up the offer extended by the Chief Constable and all his Cheshire wizards of early retirement."

"On what grounds – Post Traumatic Stress Disorder? Or, no don't tell me, they found the box of ex-KGB electronic listening devices in a box under your desk."

"Something like that."

"Which?"

"I called a member of our illustrious legal profession an irritating little tit and he's made a complaint."

"For calling him a tit?"

"Well it might not have been in those precise words."

"Ah."

"Anyway he's taken up the cudgels and the Chief Constable …"

"And all his little wizards …"

"Are investigating his accusations and my … er … rather unorthodox methods, which, would you believe, have been castigated as straight out of the middle if not downright dark ages. So to save them all the bother I've resigned, due ill health caused by the mental stress of another investigation and I've therefore been hurriedly allocated early retirement on health grounds, thus saving a huge amount of taxpayers' money and embarrassment all round."

"But what about the er … tit?"

"I'll lurk outside his office and break both his legs and then those of his toerag client."

"Ah."

"Not that that has anything to do with it of course."

"Heaven forbid."

"Exactly."

"By unorthodox methods?"

"Dare I mention the capture of one demented druid and the demolition of half a cliffside?"

"Best to retire."

"I thought so."

"And how has Moira taken it?"

"She's drawn up a list."

"A list?"

"So far it's only two sides of A4."

"Oh dear."

"She's included a barbecue area with decking, a rose arbour, something *she* calls a gazebo and the conversion of the garage into a self contained apartment, complete with power shower and basic cooking facilities."

"How basic?"

"More than a kettle and marginally less than something Gordon Ramsay could throw a tantrum in."

"And you are here because?"

"It's Tuesday and there are currently hundreds of scary home and garden improving wrinklies fighting their way through B&Q, armed to the teeth with large trolleys and even larger sticks and I'm not including the ones manning the tills."

"Well that makes sense, but why are you really here."

"Checking."

"Checking?"

"That no one has been stupid enough to ask you anything about my dubious investigative methods."

"You may rest easy on that one. No one has asked and even if they did I wouldn't answer. My lips, as they say, are most firmly sealed, besides which I could hardly tell them the truth, could I?"

"Well no, not without a course of therapy and the application of a very tight white coat with extra strong buckles."

"Not forgetting the padded room and the free application of electrodes."

Bob nodded in agreement and took another reviving swallow of caffeine.

"Besides which I doubt very much if talking to dead people qualifies as a minor mental aberration," she added upon due consideration.

"... to say nothing of conversing with supernatural entitics on a daily basis," Bob agreed with a grin.

"So you've retired?" Tavistock finally asked after a moment of companionable silence.

"Yep."

"Well, how is it?"

"At first it was really great, like being on holiday, but last week I woke up, realised I didn't have to go in and face the usual crimewave of paper and nearly cried."

"Ah."

"Nobody tells you that it's so boring."

"I see."

"I thought you might, you being a mother and all."

Tavistock glared at him and Bob, sensing the tactical error, tried to retrieve his position by digging himself an even deeper verbal hole. "I mean, being stuck at home bored out of your mind with housework and small children is why you started writing, isn't it?"

"I suppose so," Tavistock grudgingly agreed.

"You told me that your brain was turning to mush and that you were becoming a daytime television addict, remember."

"So I started bumping people off in my spare time," Tavistock chuckled.

"I still remember that bit where they found the body in the frozen food section," Bob grimaced.

"Ah yes, the frozen peas with extra meaty goodness."

"I was thinking more of the severed ear in the desserts, couldn't look a black forest gateau in the face for months afterwards," Bob remarked with feeling.

They sat and sipped their respective beverages. After a while Bob stretched, yawned and grabbed another digestive.

"Anyway I've decided not to convert the garage, at least not the way Moira wants it done."

"Oh."

"No, I'm going to convert it into an office instead."

"An office?"

"With facilities."

"Right." Tavistock glanced briefly at him. "You'll need a plumber."

"I know."

"Could take months."

"Yep."

"What on earth do you need an office for anyway?"

"Do you remember old Clive Corkish?"

"Wasn't he that old drinking buddy of yours? The one that got himself injured on the mountain mile a couple of years ago?"

"That's him, he was on marshalling duties when one of the riders miscalculated the turn, separated from his machine at the bend and the next thing anybody knew was that the rider was flying over the edge and the remains of the bike were ploughing into poor old Clive. Pity really, he was a jolly good little investigator, credit to the force and all that."

"Worked in the north, liked mooching about in other people's bins?"

"He got results."

"True."

"Anyway he's still in a wheelchair but he's just finished some pepped-up high tech computer course and was wondering if I fancied going into partnership with him."

"Oh God, please tell me that the pair of you aren't going all Mickey Spillane?"

"No, nothing of the kind."

"Good."

"It will be a professionally run private detective and personal security firm."

Tavistock tried not to snigger and failed miserably.

"You can laugh, but I'll have you know that we already have our first client."

"What!"

"That wiped the smile off, thought it would."

"So if you have a client and you don't need to go to B&Q why are you really here?"

"Always the negative vibes man."

"Well."

"What do you know about Lou Sphinx?"

"The television presenter?"

"That's the one."

"Well he's known as loose Sphincter in media circles, especially by members of the film crew and he's not exactly Mr Popular by all accounts. Why?"

"He's filming some supernatural ghost investigation on midsummer's eve at the Gaiety Theatre and our new firm has been asked to sort out and look after the security."

"So?"

"We may have a teeny weeny problem?"

"The ghosts have threatened industrial action if you all don't bugger off out of it?"

"Not even mildly funny."

"Well I give up then, what's the problem?"

"This." Bob passed her a slip of paper which had printed on it in large red letters the words:

Lou Sphinx is a deadman walking

"Nice."

"It arrived in his dressing room at the studio in Manchester last week – that's a copy by the way – and nobody has any idea how."

"So why is it your problem?"

"Have you any idea how easy it would be for some crackpot to get into the Gaiety, carry out his threat and then clear off, leaving me holding the body?"

"Ah."

"Emily could do it."

"But she's ten."

"Exactly!"

"So how can I help?"

"Can you get as much information as you can dig up, the juicier the better, about this Sphinx character so that at least we know where to start looking for a few suspects?"

"Ok, I'll ring Marigold at Tiger Aspect, she knows everybody's dirty laundry, having had at some point or another to wash it."

"Right." Bob sat and thoughtfully stared into his empty mug.

"More coffee?" Tavistock asked.

"What? Oh yes please if you're making it. I don't suppose …"

"What?"

"You've heard from the old man?"

Tavistock looked blankly at him.

"You know, wanders around in a brown dressing gown, badly needs a decent haircut and a shave, swears a lot and walks through walls."

"Oh that old man. No I haven't, or at least not since you saw him in the Canary Islands a couple of years ago."

"Island hasn't been the same since he went," Bob mused.

They both remembered their old friend Mannanan Mac Lir, the rather moth-eaten minor deity in charge of the Island since the incarceration of a cannibalistic serial rapist and wondered where he was.

"You know he's not been back since we blew up The Glashton," Bob stated carefully, setting his empty coffee mug down on a dog-eared magazine with a picture of David Tennant, facing down an inflated yellow maggot, on the front.

"I wondered if that had meant that his job of protection

was finally over and he could then potter off to wherever it is that Gods potter to when they no longer belong."

"He could just have gone off on holiday," Bob mused.

"For four years?" scoffed Tavistock.

"Ah well, it was just a thought."

They sat in a pensive silence broken by a large tabby cat that emerged slowly from behind the sofa and then, after stalking across the lounge, sat under the window sill and meowed piteously until Tavistock got up and opened the window for it.

"You know, sometimes I actually miss the mad old coot," Tavistock observed, closing the window and adjusting the ornaments that the aged feline had disturbed in its urgent lunge into the leafy garden.

"So do I."

"Fresh coffee?"

"Please."

"And then you can tell me all about this new venture of yours."

"Why? So you can use it in some daft book."

"As if."

Eventually Bob ambled off to meet Clive and Tavistock went back and stared at the mound of dirty washing still adhering to the utility room floor. She sighed and went back to the lounge to clear it of crockery before starting on the laundry. It was as she was carefully rinsing coffee grounds into the waste disposal and staring out of the kitchen window at her cat that she spotted the intruder.

A large brown shaggy object had emerged from the undergrowth and was now stalking towards the family feline known affectionately as 'Killer'. Tavistock, knowing full well that the family puss was a total and utter coward, picked up a nearby jug, filled it full of cold water, and hurriedly exited to the garden, intent on letting the four-legged trespasser know in no uncertain terms that it was anything but welcome. The large, hefty dark furball regarded her with unblinking green eyes as she tossed the cold liquid over its gleaming coat. Then, to her utter astonishment, the fluid fell straight through the image of the cat and soaked the ground beneath.

"What the ..." Tavistock snapped.

"Oh there you are Claws ..." boomed a well remembered voice.

Tavistock turned to greet her old friend Mannanan and couldn't believe her eyes.

"Good Gods!" she exclaimed in astonishment.

Mannanan Mac Lir raised one eyebrow and frowned in a mocking fashion.

For instead of the scruffy unshaven Celtic look of bushy beard, matted shoulder length greying hair and dilapidated brown dressing gown with hood and cord, stood a vision of middle-aged neatness in a smart grey pinstripe suit, lavender spotted tie, spotless black patent leather shoes and designer wire-framed glasses. Mannanan slowly grinned at her, showing polished pearly white teeth, a scrupulously shaven face and a neatly understated, short haircut. Tavistock walked around him, observing the new look with a decidedly stunned demeanour.

Tavistock stopped and then sniffed suspiciously. "What is that smell?" she asked.

"What smell?" Mannanan retorted.

"Sort of clean and ... er ... faintly attractive."

"Ah that might be the Hugo Boss aftershave; I'm told it's very popular with the ladies."

"Er, right."

"So do you like the new image?"

"Um ... what was wrong with the old one?" Tavistock asked, sinking into the nearest garden chair.

"Nothing really if you happen to be into the God business, unfortunately I've retired so to speak. Well not retired really, it was more a case of seeking alternative employment commensurate with my current capabilities."

"You got the sack, didn't you?"

"Well if you insist on putting it like that, I was, as they say, let go to seek alternative employment," Mannanan grumbled as he sat himself down in a nearby chair. "And as my old job went, so as luck would have it, did the uniform and now as you see I'm dressed for civilian life."

"What, as an investment advisor, insurance salesman, or possibly, considering the tie – is that really silk?" Mannanan nodded and preened at the same time. "A double glazing salesman?"

Mannanan raised a bushy eyebrow and then, refusing to acknowledge her witticism continued unabashed, "Well to be perfectly honest I've always hankered after a smart suit and a tie. And you have no idea just how comfortable boxer shorts are, especially the silk ones."

"Whoa mister, stop right there, I'm still trying to come to terms with the fact that you're wearing glasses."

"I did consider contacts but on balance these give a more intelligent and steady image."

Tavistock choked and looked at her watch; it was only ten thirty and far too early for a drink.

"OK, let's just get this into some sort of order; you have been fired from the position of minor deity?"

"Correct."

"And you can therefore now wear whatever you want, whenever you want?"

"Again a tick in the box."

"You're still just as irritating though."

"Nobody ever said I had to do anything about the attitude."

"Right." Tavistock eyed him in a thoughtful fashion and then, feigning disinterest, asked, "So what exactly is it you *can* do?"

"Walk through walls, upset cats, dogs, small children, levitate the usual objects and slime things."

"Slime things?"

"Yes, watch." Mannanan stroked the wrought iron table top beside him and as his hand passed over the black painted surface a trail of green gunk appeared and dripped through the holes.

"George would so love that," Tavistock commented, delicately prodding the disgusting ooze with a tentative index finger. "Ugh."

"And how are the children?" Mannanan asked conversationally.

"Kate is starting her GCSE course, George is attempting to survive High school and Emily is trying to persuade her doting father that having her own pony would be a really good idea and save him lots of lovely money, as he wouldn't have to cough up the weekly riding fees although ..." Tavistock became aware of the old familiar shift in concentration and realised that Mannanan was trying to avoid something. Nobody, she thought to herself, changes that much. She smiled broadly and gave him her best Cheshire cat grin. "So why don't you tell me what you're really up to?"

"Sorry?"

"Don't give me that look, the kids do it all the time and if it doesn't work for them …"

"I have no idea what you mean," Mannanan replied, primly pursing his lips together even though his eyes twinkled behind their protective glass.

"Since when did Gods, even retired ones, need to toddle around with a briefcase?"

"Ah … thought you hadn't spotted that one."

"Eyes in the back of the head, inserted at the same time as your firstborn is released into the wild."

"Right."

"Didn't think that I'd seen you quickly hiding it behind the planter, did you?"

"That would be a definite negative on that one."

"So?"

"What?"

"Come on, I'm waiting and if necessary I can wait all day."

"Oh all right, I've got a job."

"What sort of a job?"

"Er … well … for the er … Government …"

"You a civil servant I don't think so!"

"Well I am, so there, Mrs Smarty Pants."

"Why on earth would the Government want to employ a semi-retired, thousand-year-old spook?"

"Um … well the thing is … you promise you won't tell anyone?"

Tavistock gave a resigned nod of her head and leant forward in a conspiratorial fashion. "Cross my heart and hope to expire horribly."

"There's this department within a department, or rather

underneath, in the basement, and its run by the same lot that have coordinated things down the ages."

"You mean the rumours that the elderly members of Tynwald are in fact deceased are actually true?"

"No, not the Government, the Civil Service, well not the majority of civil servants of course, just the few in the basement."

"And these … er …un-dead, they do what exactly?"

"They ensure that no spiritual activity occurs to the detriment of the tourist board."

Tavistock stared at him in mock horror. "You mean the Isle of Man Government actually employs real spooks?"

"Yes, if the occasion demands it. It's a very important jo …" Manahan's voice tailed off as Tavistock collapsed in a positive peal of giggles.

"I have now heard everything," she chortled. "You a faceless pen-pusher – do Health and Safety know?"

"No."

"I bet they don't."

"It's a job."

"Right and er … what exactly is it that you do in this er … occupation of yours?"

"I ensure that the local residents don't exceed their brief."

"And if they do? What then? Lock them up in the nearest ghostly nick and apply the red-hot pokers?"

"No, I sort any unpleasantness out, if it has occurred, and then send them up or downstairs depending on the circumstances."

"I see."

"I can send people on, you know, and not many can do that properly. It's an art."

"OK. This conversation is getting so unreal I may need

medication of an alcoholic kind at any moment."

"Well don't let me stop you; I only came round to let you know that I'm back."

"And don't think I don't appreciate it. By the way, I saw Bob this morning."

"Oh yes, and how was the miserable old sod?"

"Miserable. Actually to be fair he wasn't really that bad."

"Oh."

"No. Why don't you go and have a nice long chat?"

"Oh I couldn't interrupt him at work, you know how upset he gets with my sitting on filing cabinets and walking through the corridors, literally speaking."

"Er yes, well, he did mention that once or twice, still I'm sure that he'd like to see you and if you're lucky you should find him at home."

"At home?"

"In the garage."

"The garage?"

"Doing a spot of conversion work with large power tools and unspeakably bad language."

"I see." Mannanan watched her suspiciously. "What's the catch?"

"What catch?"

"All right, joke then."

"No joke, no catch, just pick up the briefcase and that furball cat of yours and go see good old Uncle Bob."

"He won't mind my turning up then?"

"Oh no, not at all, in fact I'd say he'd be overjoyed."

Claws waddled across the lawn, and arriving at Mannanan's feet collapsed gracelessly to one side and began licking the long fur covering her large and expansive stomach. Mannanan wasn't too sure if Bob Callow would be overjoyed by a visit but he had a job to do, his first in fact and Bob Callow might be very useful in ensuring a satisfactory conclusion. However as he was about to leave he looked down on Tavistock's tousled head and asked, "Are you still able to see things?"

"You mean are the old intuitive and psychic juices still flowing?"

"Yes."

"Absolutely – and very useful they are too when writing the dreadful stuff I still write."

"Good, good."

"Why?"

"No reason, just making polite conversation."

"Polite conversation? Since when were you even vaguely civil?"

"Ah, is that the time? Must be off, toodle pip."

And with that Mannanan vanished as swiftly as he'd appeared, together with Claws the cat, the briefcase and the faint aroma of soap and expensive designer aftershave.

Tavistock stared at the space he'd briefly occupied and gave herself a little shake. What, she thought to herself, is he really up to, and more importantly should she warn Bob?

Warm sunshine filtered through a break in the massed clouds above her head, bluebells dipped and bobbed in a light breeze as did the encroaching ring of bindweed and buttercups.

She wondered briefly about the wisdom of wielding a large fork and attacking the unwanted foliage before it got any worse and then her stomach growled in protest. "Feed me, feed me now," it bellowed.

"Maybe later," she thought, ambling back inside. "After chocolate ... lots and lots of chocolate ... and a long and gossipy phone call to Marigold."

* * *

Richard Allan, accountant, senior civil servant and husband to the afore-mentioned, well known local author, Tavistock Allan, sat in his Douglas office and surveyed the list of names in front of him with something akin to panic. If he got it wrong he would be hung, drawn and quartered by the local press but on the other hand if he got it right feathers would be ruffled for years, "Mind you," he reassured himself, "it would make the sending out of the Christmas cards a hell of a lot cheaper."

He took a deep breath, cleared his throat and picked up the telephone.

"Ah Sarah, er is that you? ... right ... well ... er ... could you go and get mummy for me please ... It's Richard ... Richard Allan the Director ... yes you got a part ... The maid Edith ... oh yes, it's a smashing little role and quite spooky in places ... The first rehearsal starts promptly at seven in the church hall, the one opposite the post office ... OK, bye then, see you tonight."

He put down the phone muttered "Well that was easy" and crossed Sarah Corkill's name off the list in front of him with a flourish. He toyed with the idea of having at least a stiff drink before phoning the next member of the cast but resisted the urge in favour of a large espresso.

It took a while to get connected as the next closet thespian was in the process of changing a barrel and had to be located by one of the many young men she habitually employed as temporary bar staff, all of whom were noted more for their six-pack physique than cognitive thought.

After a while a deep voice barked abrasively down the

telephone line, "Ah Richard – and about bloody time – so I got the part did I?"

Richard took a deep breath and doodled a large circle on the pad in front of him with a knife in the centre of it.

"Well yes and no. No because you didn't get the part of Elvira and yes because you did get Ruth … Because Elvira has to be young and girly and you are a strapping example of womanhood in its prime … No I didn't say that you were too fat … Or too old … Oh don't be silly, Frances is young and a jolly good little actress if she remembers to speak up … Because you are on stage for most of the first half of the play and I need someone with a forceful Thatcher-type personality … Marianna I did not say that … For God's sake woman, if you don't want the part say so as I'm sure that young Jules would jump at the chance … Exactly, and you can bring a wealth of expertise to the entire play, which reminds me I haven't picked Colin for the part of Charles … because Terry told me he had already auditioned for Pirates and got a main role … For Heaven's sake put that libido of yours aside for just one moment, if he does both plays it will be last July all over again, Oh I know, I know … Anyway I'd better go, I'll see you tonight then, at seven prompt to start blocking the First Act and we can discuss costumes and changes then …"

Richard sighed and very carefully disconnected. Marianna was a very good actress but how anyone could possibly think of her as the play's sexy piece was beyond him, especially as she had the face and body of an upmarket Hyacinth Bouquet and the abrasive personality of pumice with a tendency to explode at regular intervals.

John Smith and Eve Saunders who he had decided would be an excellent pairing as Dr and Mrs Bradman were next and so he left a message on their shared answer machine. They had recently moved in together after meeting up on a walk organized by a local singles club, which his wife had cruelly although aptly named the Nutters' Nookery. Both were divorced, both had an interest in amateur dramatics and both would be perfect for the husband and wife roles, which would only require them to learn lines similar to the ones they habitually used and to be themselves.

Next was the turn of local decorator and part-time radio presenter Geoff Caine. Richard waited patiently as the receptionist at Manx Radio tried vainly and at great length to find him but in the end left a message for him to turn up as soon as he could at the church hall.

Stella Corlett answered almost immediately and gushed her thanks as Richard vainly tried to get a word in edgeways, sideways or anyways. Stella, a local herbalist and well known exponent of the acupuncture needle positively purred down the line until Richard firmly shouted 'I'll see you at seven then,' and hastily rang off. Stella might be a little deaf and very dotty but she aced cameo parts and would be brilliant as the eccentric and totally incompetent medium.

Frances Myers would still be somewhere within the confines of the Isle of Man College and so he left a message with her proud mother, and then after ensuring that Mary Skillicorn was willing to hunt down the props and that her partner Harvey was able to find the time to redesign and paint the set, which he kept in a lock-up in Onchan, Richard laid the steaming instrument of communication to cool down and went in search of an early lunch and Marks & Spencer socks.

★ ★ ★

Mannanan Mac Lir surveyed the newly plastered cellar with a cynical eye and wrote something in a neat gothic script upon the paper attached to his Isle of Man Government issue clipboard.

A shadow which had been prowling down the stairwell towards him stopped, picked up a small piece of unidentified builder's rubbish and threw it at him. Mannanan looked up and the missile promptly exploded harmlessly a foot away from him.

"Ah," Mannanan barked. "I wondered when you'd turn up."

The shadow froze and then muttered darkly to itself, the prevailing consonants being 'f', 'b' and 's' and most of them ended in 'ing'.

"I presume that you must be Bartholomew, commonly known as Barty, West, late of this address," Mannanan enquired, flicking over a couple of pages, his glasses glinting as he moved.

"And what if it is?" a voice hissed.

"Well if it is, I have to advise you of your rights."

"My what?"

"Your rights as an injured spirit."

"Injured, I was bleedin' killed mate!"

"Exactly." Mannanan fixed him with a steely and steady eye and waited as Barty West reluctantly materialised. Barty glared belligerently up at him and reminded Mannanan forcibly of a bad tempered garden gnome in a suit.

"Well that certainly explains the poltergeist activity without the full emanation," Mannanan observed, ticking one of the boxes on his list.

"Do soddin' wot?" Barty asked and angrily bobbed up and down.

"Well considering your obvious lack of inches and resemblance to a popular garden ornament, materialisation in your case would not have resulted in terrified screams but loud and raucous laughter."

"Are you trying to be f'ing funny mate?" Barty asked, advancing towards Mannanan with his hands clenched into two bony fists.

"Oh no, I'm never funny," Mannanan answered and then as if coming to a decision put the clipboard down on a convenient pile of sand and smiled. It wasn't in any way a nice or friendly smile and it certainly had no intention of ever reaching his eyes, which began to glow a fierce and fiery red.

Barty West, sensing that he had made some sort of tactical error stepped back a pace.

"Now you listen to me, you horrible little entity, I have just about had my fill of rude and foul-mouthed little squibs like you and if you say one more word ending with 'ing' I will send you on to the next stage of your miserable little afterlife without a backward glance, I'll even forge your signature on the acceptance form."

Barty gulped and lowered his eyes. "Sorry," he grunted, looking down at his stockinged feet.

Mannanan followed his gaze and sighed "And what," he asked in sepulchral tones, "have you done with your shoes?"

"Me? I did nuffink I did, some bast   Somebody took 'em, that's what 'appened."

"Oh."

"Knocked me over the back of the head wiv a spade and nicked me ... ing shoes, leather they was too and almost new."

"Ah, so you were murdered?"

"Well I didn't hit meself over the back of the head and bury meself in cement, did I?"

"I hope that was a rhetorical question?"

"Do wot?"

"Never mind." Mannanan took a deep breath and beckoned the clipboard to him by crooking his index finger in a weary fashion. The board flew up and into his hand and Barty, not easily impressed, had to admit that he was. He was also, even though he hated to acknowledge it, even a little afraid of the tall gentleman in the pristine pinstripe suit in the way that his lawyer and accountant had terrified him during his lifetime.

"Barty West, I am hereby authorised by the Manx Government to offer you redress for your previous injuries by way of divine retribution, or if you prefer by offering you a deluxe package to your preferred afterlife."

"Er …"

"To put it bluntly, you can either set in motion the means of catching your killer or you can move on, but what you cannot do is to continue with your previous childish activities and frighten off the few remaining out of season tourists that we currently have."

"And wot if I say stuff you?" Barty hissed.

"Then I will have great pleasure in sending you on somewhere cold, dark and infinitely lonely."

"Like where f'rinstance?"

"How about deep space?"

"I've always liked the stars."

"But possibly not the big black bits in between and not for eternity or until the next Big Bang."

"Well no, possibly not, how about coming back as summat else? Like wot them Indians do?"

"Well, I suppose we could do something on those lines …"

"Good. I fancy coming back as summat big and mean – or even better how about one of them models wiv the big tits?"

"Page three type?"

"That's the ticket – now you're talking."

"There is only one problem with that as far as I can see …"

"Wot problem?"

"You apparently have to have earned the points in your last life to entitle you to fame fortune and big …"

"Knockers?"

"I was going to say rewards."

"Right, so what could I come back as?"

Mannanan consulted one of the lists attached to the board and smiled, this time with his eyes as well as his mouth.

"I could do you a nice earthworm, or how about a garden slug? The lifespan isn't much but at least no one will eat you and if you're very lucky you'll fall in an organic beer trap and die a happy little inebriated invertebrate."

"Oh." Barty swallowed before whining in a plaintive fashion, "I wasn't that bad."

"No?"

"No."

"Dare I mention that business over the substandard housing in Brighton? The theft of several offshore funds, the holiday business that left 250 stranded in Benidorm and the Chinese restaurant in Bootle?"

"Ah."

"Yes, ah, and those were only the ones we had room for

on the form. Frankly I think I'm being generous with the offer of the earthworm because if I had my way you'd have difficulty racking up enough points for the average amoeba."

"Couldn't I just stay as I am?"

"No."

"And what if I refuse to do or sign any fink? After all you can't make me go. I mean to say, wot are you anyway, a jumped-up little clerk, a proverbial pen-pusher? Bet you never ever did anything out of the ordinary, did you eh? Bet you never said boo to the proverbial goose, did ya eh, eh?"

Mannanan grinned and then thought to himself, "I am really, really, going to enjoy this."

"So you want to know who I am, do you?" Mannanan asked.

Barty nodded smugly.

Mannanan clapped his hands and then seemed to grow taller, the suit faded to be replaced by his old robes which now glittered as if they were sprinkled in rhinestones. Barty watched in mounting horror as the clipboard disappeared to be replaced in Mannanan's hands by a long and evil-looking staff around which a large and ugly dragon writhed.

"My name is Mannanan Mac Lir, I have killed many men in defence of this Isle during my lifetime and even more during my death and I have seen more evil than you could ever have imagined."

"Mannanan, but you're a God or a myth or something …" Barty whimpered as he was picked up as if by giant invisible hands and was then spun sickeningly around the confined cellar space.

"Or something …" Mannanan reiterated.

"Look, I'm sorry all right, I got it wrong, could you pleeze just put me down or make it stop or summat only I haven't felt anything for thirty-odd years and now I feel really, really sick."

Mannanan stopped him spinning by the simple expedient of plucking him from the air and planting him feet first on the newly laid concrete floor.

Claws the cat ambled from the shadows and looked up at Barty West with her tongue hanging out.

"On the other hand I could make an exception and allow you a brief spell on earth as a mouse, although the life expectancy might be shorter than usual," Mannanan advised him with a grin.

Barty West looked down at the cat and shivered. "Er, no thanks, if it's all the same to you, I'd like to just stay on until you can sort out a bit of vengeance and retribution. That is if you think I deserve it."

"I suppose so, after all nobody really deserves to be murdered, even you."

"Er, fanks, I fink."

"So do you know who it was that terminated your life span?"

"Er, no."

"No?"

"No, I wasn't looking you see, I was inspectin' the concrete footins, next fing I know wos whack and then nothing but blackness until they dug me up."

"Umm, right, well then ... if I find out who killed you and arrange for them to be hauled in front of a judge will you agree to journey on to the next level?"

"Couldn't I help?"

"Help?"

"As your assistant?"

"Assistant!"

"Yeah a sort of PA as it were, I could fetch and carry and ..." Barty looked desperately around and then down.

"I could feed the cat."

"That was I think my previous suggestion?"

"Er, yes, but by feed I meant open a tin or summat."

There was a pause followed by a lengthy silence. After what seemed like hours Mannanan appeared to have come to a decision.

"All right, you can help me with my enquiries but first ..."

"Yes?"

"We are going back to the office to procure you a pair of shoes."

Chapter Two

"Mr West, your advocate is on the line."

Bartholomew West, entrepreneur and the Island's Business Man of the Year, for the years 1997 and 2001 heaved himself towards his desk and picked up the phone.

"Ah, Tony, how are you? ... Good, good ... and that delightful young wife of yours? ... And your two lovely children? Better and better ... so, so, you know how it is ... Now Tony, what I want to ask you is this, hypothetically speaking and we are only speaking hypothetically, if someone was to enquire after the state of my companies and in particular our silent parent company what exactly would you have to tell them? ... I see ... well of course you would, no question about it there ... can't have a member of the Manx bar not behaving in a right and proper fashion ... no, no particular reason ... and I presume that everything is now computerised ... did you really ... well, well who would have thought it, eh? ... even the old files in the basement? Well well, I suppose it's progress ... I know a long time, almost ... well it must be more than thirty years now

… Of course I remember you were articled to … now who was it … thin weedy chap with those odd glasses, used to fly Spitfires in the war … Ah well, now the reason I was phoning was because Arthur is liquidating a few things before my retirement, and … well, yes I know, but as you can't take it with you I thought I'd have a couple of years really enjoying the stuff, after all if I leave it to the kids they'll only spend it! … Just a joke Tony, just a joke, there are still those innumerable trusts you and that partner of yours persuaded me to set up … ah Tony, must go, I have another call on the line … yes indeed next Thursday then 12.30 at Ciappelli's." He pressed his finger down firmly on one of the many buttons and disconnected, frowning as he redialled and waited before speaking again.

"Haslett? Its me, West. I have a little job for you, well two little jobs really. Firstly I want you to find me a hacker, a really good one and I want this virtual crook to go into the computer programmes of my accountant and my lawyer … because I want all my company files deleted or scrambled in such a way that they will be totally and utterly useless … I have no idea … I'll pay up to three thousand for instant professional results … I'll give him all the account names and numbers but I want the lot corrupted, nothing else, just them … because by the time anyone notices anything wrong I will have left the Island, leaving no forwarding address. One last thing – my lawyer, Tony Banks – I want him taken out of the equation for a bit, nothing fancy, just put the frighteners on him … use his family if necessary and watch it, I have a feeling that things could go very bad if we don't tread very carefully … exactly. Oh and in future I'll contact you on the secure line don't ring me here or on the mobile. Of course, funds to the usual account and tell Simon that I may need to use the boat."

"Mr West, your letters ... and your wife is downstairs," his secretary stated as she approached his large and cluttered leather-topped antique desk

"What the hell does she want?"

"I have no idea Sir, perhaps you could ask her," his secretary muttered as she handed over a wad of letters with their attached notes and cheques.

"One day," she thought, "one day I'm going to win the Lottery, not a lot but maybe just enough to enable me to tell you just exactly where you can stick your loathsome job, and believe me Sir when I say that you'll need more than a tube of haemorrhoid cream and a rubber ring for comfort afterwards."

She smiled briefly at the mere thought of it and then collecting all the signed documents, hurriedly left his office in order to avoid the gormless plastic Mrs West and her infuriating girly Essex voice wheedling yet more money from her doting elderly spouse.

* * *

Bob Callow and Clive Corkish sat amidst the usual detritus found lurking in the average garage and drank tea in a companionable silence as they contemplated their future workspace with identical thought-filled grins. Bob was perched on an upturned plastic tool box; whilst Clive lolled comfortably in his wheelchair. Bob Callow, middle-aged, with a girth to match and a good deal less hair than he liked, poked a cardboard box with his foot. It rattled dully. Idly he wondered what on earth it contained and if he'd get much at the next car boot sale.

Clive was having similar thoughts about a set of concrete

garden pigs he'd hidden in his own glory hole. Clive was around the same age as Bob but a good deal fitter and thinner. His skin was tanned and dark olive in colour and his hair curled in short dark whorls emphasising the fact that his paternal grandfather had originated from an obscure part of Southern Italy, although his accent was pure Ramsey.

"We could do a lot with this," Clive stated, taking another sip of tea. "We stick a window and a door where the garage door is now, a toilet over there in the corner near the boiler and a smallish kitchenette with sink over near the side window."

"Which is exactly what I've got on the plans," Bob crowed, handing them over.

"Problem is, what do we do until they get approved and we find a builder?" Clive asked.

"Got a builder, old Juan Duggan, same chap that did the conservatory and the kitchen extension."

"I thought he'd retired."

"He did, well he sold up to his son but as far as I can tell he still supervises on a daily basis."

"Must drive the poor little sod mad."

"It does, mind you as young Ian doesn't know his footings from his elbow perhaps it's a good thing old Juan didn't amble off to sunny Spain."

"Well good news for us, not for Jean though."

"Poor Jean."

"She's still in remission though, isn't she?"

"Last I heard, yes."

"Good, nice lady that."

"One of the best, taught our eldest how to split the atom."

"Always a useful attribute that. By the way how's he doing down under?"

"All right as far as we know, got a contract with the Australian navy servicing computers on submarines."

"Submarines, eh? Rather him than me."

"Anyway we'll know in November when we go out for the wedding."

"Nice girl is she?"

"Nurse."

"Come in useful when they have kids."

"Ah well, time for that sort of thing when they've got a house and everything, only renting at the moment as he moves about a bit. Mind you whenever I ring he always seems to be burning shrimp and opening cans!"

"Ah, the good life."

"Speaking of which we need to draw up some sort of partnership agreement and get some insurance."

"Bank account, letterheads and cards, desk, office equipment, and not forgetting the computer."

"Do we have to have one?"

"Yes Bob we do, and one with a proper printer, and a website. We could also get one of them digital cameras for surveillance and a few hand held electronic listening devices."

"Don't they have those technical exhibitions where you can buy all sorts of stuff?"

"State of the art, bug anything, anywhere, any time."

"And not just the holding cells in the old prison?"

"And we don't get investigated for using them!"

"Well, not much."

They sat in a contemplative and companionable silence whilst somewhere in the distance the sound of a washing machine reaching its final cycle could be clearly heard.

"Still, that's all behind us now. By the way, did I tell you that we've got our first job?" Bob said searching for the crumpled letter still residing in one of his many pockets.

"Really?"

"Yeah. Phoenix Television wants us to protect one of their most infamous presenters, apparently he's been receiving death threats."

"Oh, which presenter?"

"Lou Sphinx."

"Good grief, not that obnoxious red-haired twit with the weasel features and irritating taste in designer shirts?"

"The very same."

"Goes about scaring the paying viewer by visiting haunted houses in the dark with very small torches and even smaller cameras?"

"So you do watch it?"

"Who doesn't? Actually I rather like the batty old barmpot."

"You must be one of the few that do then, as somebody, somewhere, dislikes him enough to be a regular correspondent and knows him well enough to get quite personal."

"Lets have a squiz then."

Bob handed over the letter and a plastic-covered sheaf of notes, all written in red on what looked suspiciously like old-fashioned hard toilet paper.

"I didn't think they made this stuff any more," Clive stated, gingerly turning the plastic over so that he could see the back.

"That's not blood is it?" He asked with a note of distaste.

"Windsor and Newton, pillar box red."

"Very artistic."

"The first one said he was a dead man walking. The

second note got very anatomical if not downright obscene and the third was just, well … barmy."

"All by the same person?"

"Apparently so. All of them were hand delivered to his dressing room by being pushed under the door, no prints, no markings, no dried fluids, nothing traceable to anywhere or anything, not even an envelope."

"Weird."

"To be honest I thought it might have been some sick joke except for two things."

"Which were?"

"Somebody cut the brakeline on his car, which luckily for him was spotted by an eagle-eyed security guard in the car park, or at least the leaking fluid was."

"And the second?"

"He always has vodka after each recording and somebody left him a bucket of ice and ground glass to go with it."

"Good grief!"

"As luck would have it the programme was cancelled due to unspecified technical difficulties and nobody went back to the dressing rooms until the next day."

"So who found the doctored ice?"

"A cleaner, unfortunately she helped herself to a drink, vodka and orange with lots of ice and ended up in hospital with suspected appendicitis. They found the glass in her stomach when running initial tests and managed to pump most of it out; she's still not a well lady by all accounts."

"Vicious bastard."

"And I would say ever so slightly insane."

"So why call us, why not the police?"

"Do you remember my old mate Greg?"

"Manchester CID."

"That's him; he's retired now, runs his own firm out at Barton near the airfield, anyway he knows the producer and because they're next filming a special over here, put my – or rather our – names forward."

"And the next thing you know it's a case of Bob's your Uncle."

"We are really going to have to instigate a few ground rules about naff jokes."

"Sorry, just slipped out, as the actress said to the bishop."

"Clive."

"Yes mate?"

"Shut up!"

"So what do we do?"

"Well I thought we could have a look around the sites they are to visit over here and get as much information about the studio personnel and this guy Sphinx."

"Sounds a good place to start. By the way, what was the technical difficulty?"

"Something to do with a flooded cellar but I'll find out more when Greg potters over."

"He's coming across?"

"Tomorrow. The plan is that I pick him up from Ronaldsway Airport and ferry him down to the Sefton Hotel."

"Cor, posh."

"Budget special rates by courtesy of Tourism and the Film board."

"Our taxes paying for more jollies."

"And our fees."

"Ah well, it's not all bad then."

"Not this time around, no. Anyway, I'll settle him in and

then you join us for coffee and a chat about three?"

"Sounds fine by me."

Clive banged his mug down on a nearby paint can and manoeuvred himself to the garage door, which Bob then opened with an electronic gizmo he'd found earlier in a box of assorted computer wires and domestic appliance innards.

He pocketed the black plastic brick with a grin; he was finally getting to grips with this private enterprise thing and he had the distinct feeling that working outside the box was going to be more fun than he'd had for ages.

Bob Callow was still grinning when he heard the knock on the side door to the garage, a smile which froze rigid on seeing who it actually was.

"Bloody Norah!" Bob exclaimed. "I thought you were a double glazing salesman."

Mannanan Mac Lir frowned. "It's the briefcase, isn't it?"

"Er and the suit, the non hairy visage and the fact that you appear to have recently washed."

"Ah."

"Bet the lice were really pleased."

"May I come in?" Mannanan asked, icily ignoring the remark.

"Oh right sorry, I guess that walking through walls in your normal fashion doesn't quite go with the new image."

"No."

"So what do you think?"

"About what?"

"All this?" Bob exclaimed throwing his arms out wide and including all parts of the neon lit cluttered and grimy space.

"It's a garage." Mannanan observed. "And not a particularly clean one."

"Ignore the grime."

"That may be difficult."

Bob glowered at Mannanan and shook his head in mock sorrow. "Where is your vision, where the avid imagination?"

Mannanan took a slight step backwards and regarded him in the way you would a large dog with foam around its mouth, after all how many canines actually eat soap?

"This, my old friend, is going to be the pulsing heart of Callow and Corkish, detective and security agency."

"Do you get a fedora hat, a large black car and a secretary with all the necessary accoutrements?" Mannanan asked in an interested fashion.

"Accoutrements?"

"One hundred words a minute and a forty-two D bust?"

"Blonde?"

"Of course."

"Er no, but I do get a new computer and as many electronics gizmos as the company can afford and the bank will agree to."

"You don't actually ask for funding of illegal bugging equipment, surely!" Mannanan asked in shocked tones.

"No, it's called office equipment and sundry items."

"And this will be the nerve centre?"

"Eventually. Big window there, desk here, filing cabinets there and in the corner tea- and coffee-making facilities."

"You'll need a plumber."

"Unfortunately, yes."

"Could take months."

"Have you been talking to Tavistock?" Bob asked, seating himself back down on the handy plastic toolbox which was beginning to show the early signs of stress. Mannanan continued to wander at will investigating and prodding as he went.

"She thought it would be in my interest to have a chat."

"Why?"

"She's a woman so who knows?"

"True, very true. So how goes it in the world of myth and legend?"

"I was offered early retirement on the grounds of expediency."

"Which means what exactly?"

"To be honest I have no idea really, although allowing murder and mayhem to occur on my patch at all too frequent intervals didn't do the CV a lot of good."

"Or losing half a cliff face?"

"Er no. So what about you?"

"Early retirement on health grounds." Mannanan stared at him blankly so with a sigh Bob added, "Post Traumatic Stress Disorder."

"Ah."

"All those bodies and my unorthodox methods didn't help."

"Unorthodox?"

"Talking to dead people like you!"

"But you got results," Mannanan remarked.

"Aye, unfortunately the powers that be also want at least half a rain forest of correctly completed forms, with all boxes ticked and all legal potholes well and truly filled."

"I wouldn't have put you down as a forms man."

"Neither did they, hence the change of office. Mind you after the initial shock it was fun to start with," Bob mused, rubbing a stubbly chin.

"All that free time, no pressing need to actually get up and do anything." Mannanan agreed, remembering his stint as a retired God, third-class.

"Bloody boring after a while," Bob remarked, remembering the interminable hours sitting in Tesco's car park waiting for Moira to finish the shopping, and then the queue in B&Q afterwards on the way home and as for the garden centres, even the simple word 'Eden' could bring on palpitations.

"And you get asked to really awful parties with people you never liked in the first place and they moan at you if you don't go for being a miserable old git and ..."

"When you do go they call you a party pooper for still being miserable."

"You too?"

"Oh yes."

Bob suddenly brightened and rubbed his hands together as he remembered all the most recent invitations he'd turned down due to his new occupation and grinned.

"Still, with this new firm all that's a thing of the past. Anyway that's more than enough about me, what are you up to now?"

"Me?"

"The new image, suit and ... er ... is that your cat?"

"Cat?"

"Great big evil-eyed fluffy brown thing with no visible tail?"

"Claws. Found her one Christmas Eve wandering around the underbrush, seemed her people had moved off Island leaving her with the neighbours and their children from hell, she left one dark and rainswept evening by prising open the basement window and had lived rough until the winter set in and she died. Of course being a true Manx she'd worked out that she'd been shortchanged on the living bit and refused to move on so I adopted her and we've been together ever since. To be honest, it's been nice having the company although even I have to admit that she's not one for in-depth conversations, it's more, food, sleep, kill, eat, sleep, food, scratch."

"Er no, not exactly erudite."

"She has a nice deep purr though especially if you rub her tummy."

"Right." Bob watched the cat sniffing suspiciously at a cardboard box; she then pushed her head through the fabric of the box itself and in the process frightened a solitary mouse to death. The astonished rodent had nanoseconds to think 'Oops' before its ectoplasmic body was bitten in half and eaten. Claws withdrew her shaggy head and licked her lips in a somewhat satisfied fashion.

Bob shook his head and fixed his attention onto the briefcase that Mannanan had carefully placed by his feet.

"So what exactly is it that you do then? I mean now that you are out of the God business?"

"Oh not much really … Actually I was wondering if you could help me clear up a few loose ends, so to speak?"

"Such as?"

"Ever heard of a chap called Bartholomew or Barty West?"

"No. Why?"

"No reason really, it's just that his name has cropped up recently on something I was working on."

"Working on?"

"A couple of flats, holiday accommodation, several unhappy tourists and a suddenly absent landlord."

"Bartholomew West."

"I see you haven't lost your touch, detective."

"Once learnt never forgotten."

"Umm."

"So what did this West character do?"

"He died."

"Ah."

"Thirty years ago. Unfortunately according to his bank he's still running the aforementioned apartments and various current and deposit accounts."

"Ah, I see, and you would like me to find out how?"

"If you wouldn't mind. As I say, Barty is now resigned to the fact that he is unhappily dead, but would like to know why his empire, such as it was, is still up and running with his signature still on all the cheques, including I might add the one for the cleaner which he apparently signed himself, last Friday."

"How did he die?"

"He was whacked over the back of the head with a spade and then his assailant thoughtfully covered him in cement, a tastefully laid tin sheet and matching floor covering."

"Who?"

"He has absolutely no idea but has agreed that if I find out he will be happy to pass on to the next plane and to stop throwing objets d'art at the tourists."

"Well, I'll rattle a few boxes and see what falls out and … er … you might be able to help me in return."

"Ah … I see … there is, I believe, no such thing as a free lunch."

"Exactly." Mannanan and Bob smiled conspiratorially at each other.

"All right, what do you want?"

"What I want is information."

"About what?"

"Any spectral shenanigans currently going on at the Gaiety Theatre." Bob stopped grinning and watched uncertainly as Mannanan with a sigh seated himself on a large upturned planter.

"How long have you got?" Mannanan asked. "Because this may take some time."

* * *

The long metal barrel with its accompanying silencer, automatic night sight and carefully packed bullets lay surrounded by other weapons of mass destruction and was almost indistinguishable from the hamper's bona fide artificial replicas. White twisted blobs of spongy polystyrene were wedged further in and then a handful more were thrown on top of the plastic and metal shapes.

"There, that should do it." One of the three shadowed packers announced.

"Do you have the label?" the shortest of the trio asked, bending over the wicker basket.

"Here," the tallest said, and thrust a stiff piece of card forward, where it was carefully inspected in the white glare of a wavering torch.

The lid was firmly pushed down, the leather belt and buckles were correctly tied and the label attached with a length of thick green nylon string. The label stated quite firmly that it was a consignment of props and other theatrical devices and that its destination was 'The Middling Players c/o The Gaiety Theatre, Harris Promenade, Douglas, Isle of Man.'

Slowly all three conspirators pushed and pulled it to one

side of the room where it was carefully placed amongst other identical baskets, all labelled with the same address and all containing nothing more lethal than an assortment of wigs and set costume pieces together with a large crystal ball and a trick table.

Chapter Three

The large, expensively maintained house squatted comfortably next to its neighbours and looked with light-rimmed windows towards the sea. A manicured lawn bejewelled with lush, bright borders of blowsy poppies and upright irises bobbed and ducked in a gentle breeze. A children's plastic swing swung silently and the abandoned trampoline made strange noises as if an invisible and miniscule orchestra were tuning up.

Inside the house a restless pacing figure could be seen silhouetted against the bespoke blinds. The shadow stopped abruptly and then, as it turned back into the centre of the room, vanished. Inside the house the occupants, a young mother and her two small children waited. Food congealed gently on plates scarcely touched and the kettle cooled in a corner of the granite-topped kitchen, an Earl Grey tea bag and its unfilled mug now temporarily forgotten amidst the clutter

The woman looked anxiously at the telephone before picking the receiver up and then having second or even third thoughts, put it back down with gently shaking hands. Her two small children stood in front of her and silently watched.

A clock ticked in the hall behind them and then loudly pinged the hour.

She sighed; it was now or never and despite the gravest misgivings she picked up the phone once more and pressed the buttons.

"Is that Isla?" she asked, a faint tremor in her well modulated voice.

"Yes," came the terse reply.

"Can I please speak to Alex?"

"No."

"Oh."

"He's out." There was the sound of slurping and then a pause followed by a metallic click.

"Look, I hate to bother you …"

"Then don't!"

"Please, please don't hang up, I really, really need your help …" The younger woman's voice broke and she sobbed bitterly.

"Oh God, not another one," Isla growled as another shirt joined the others in the gently smoking metal bin at her feet. "What did he do? Promise undying love or … please tell me you're not pregnant?"

"Pregnant?"

"Best years of my life I gave that two-timing bastard and what does he do? Well I'll tell you, shall I? He sodding waits until the day of our silver wedding anniversary and announces that he did love me very much but he doesn't any more because he's going to be a daddy, as if the lack of progeny was my fault and then and then …"

"What?"

"He buggers off to Benidorm with some mousy secretary, thirty years his junior who he says is with child! His child!"

"Alex?"

"Yes."

"Oh." Jemima Banks tried hard to imagine the portly form of Alexander Fitzhammond having extra marital sex with anyone and gave up; it was like trying to imagine Rumpole of the Bailey naked.

"Anyway," Isla barked. "Who are you?"

"It's Jemima, Jemima Banks, Tony's wife."

"Banks, Banks … junior partner, plays golf … badly …"

"Yes."

"Oh … well, what do you want?"

"Well I really needed to speak to Alex, but I can tell that this isn't a good time. I mean I wouldn't normally have rung but in the circumstances I thought I'd better before ringing the police …" One of the children tucked a small hand in her free one and squeezed it hard.

There was the smallest of pauses and the sound of something gently sizzling.

"Perhaps I can help?" Isla lit a cigarette from the spiralling flames with the smoking remains of her errant husband's golf club membership forms, including his jealously guarded card for the Royal Golf Club at St Andrews and took a long hard drag on the resulting Sobranie fumes. She exhaled with a twisted smile and then added a pair of hand-tooled leather shoes and an expensive set of putters to the conflagration.

"Well, it's just that Tony hasn't come home yet … and I wouldn't ring but he promised to let me know if he was going out to lunch, so I could get him something if he wasn't and he never rang me back. And he forgot to pick the children up after swimming club and he never, ever forgets that." Jemima, realising with a start that she was babbling, abruptly stopped and caught her breath.

"I see." There was a pause on the other end of the line as Isla took another gulp of neat vodka.

"Isla, are you still there?"

"He hasn't contacted you at all?"

"No, and it's getting so late I had to pick the children up myself and I looked behind the office and his car was still there but none of the lights were on."

"Ah … Look Jemima, seeing as it's Tony, who I do remember now I come to think about it, as one of the most boring of prematurely old farts and one that even I couldn't imagine running off with a dead chicken let alone a live secretary."

Jemima gave a small insulted gasp but waited nonetheless for Isla to finish her vitriolic ramble.

Isla wiped her mouth on her designer sleeve and thoughtfully added a large golden engraved cup to the bin. Finally she spoke again, her words slightly more slurred than before. "If you like I'll ring around and try and get hold of Alex or someone, after all I still have Daddy's shares in the firm and if he thinks … Anyway I shall let you know, in the meantime I would advise you to have a large gin and stop worrying. Have you rung the hospital?"

"Not yet."

"Well I would, after all he could have just fallen over and got run down by a little man in a van."

"Oh."

"Who was the client he was having lunch with?"

"De Vannier, I think?"

"Right, I'll ring Portia, she always knows what's going on."

"Portia?"

"Reception, my eyes and ears, how else do you think I found out about that bastard's latest piece of arm candy?"

"Oh."

"I'll ring straight back," Isla promised, before disconnecting with a gentle click. On the far side of the Island Jemima sat and stared mutely at the phone.

A few minutes later Isla rang back.

"Jemima love, this may be something or nothing but Tony never turned up. I rang Portia and apparently he left the office at eleven to walk down to the restaurant and never got there, the client was understandably furious, rang her and in the end saw Sophie."

"Oh." Jemima clasped the receiver in both hands to stop the shaking and stared unseeingly at the carpet.

"Listen Jemima if I were you I'd call the police, you never know Tony may have had some sort of accident on the way and for some reason nobody has discovered who he is, although even I know that that's unlikely, especially considering the number of times he's had his face plastered all over the paper since becoming the Rotary Club's latest chairman, or should that be chairperson?"

"The police."

"I think it would be best and I'll be right over as soon as I can get a taxi, you are still out at Santon?"

"Yes."

"Lovely garden, I still remember that really super barbecue you laid on for that Swiss bank." Isla looked down at the smoking bin and then with a shrug stuffed the entire golf bag in and then for good measure the remainder of the petrol from the plastic container they used to top up the lawn mower, there was a minor explosion and a startled gasp from the other end of the phone.

"What was that noise?" Jemima asked.

"Just clearing out a few things," Isla replied, moving away from the fire and back to her house, the flames clearly reflected in the latticed panes. "I'll be with you in a tick," Isla advised.

The connection was again broken and Jemima Banks sat back on the brocade-covered sofa and shivered.

"Mum?" a tentative voice asked.

"It's all right dears, Daddy's partner's wife is coming over and I have to let the police know, Daddy's probably just had a fall or something."

"And lost his memory, you know, like the piano man," her son murmured in a bracing fashion to his younger sibling.

Jemima reached for the telephone again and dialled police headquarters; something horrible had happened and if it hadn't Tony would probably go ballistic when he found out that she had panicked and got the local constabulary involved. Jemima shuddered and then strengthening her resolve, asked to speak to someone about a missing person. "After all," she reasoned internally, "if Tony didn't want a fuss he should have at least had the decency to let me know where the hell he actually was."

* * *

Police Constable Andy Quayle looked from one anxious face to another and smiled his best and most brilliant grin.

"I'm sure that nothing bad has happened to your daddy

but I need to ask your mummy a few questions, OK?" The two children in front of him nodded seriously and his companion PC Peter Quine gave a small almost imperceptible nod to his partner and flicked open his notebook.

"Mrs Banks, or would you prefer to be called Jemima?"

"Jemima please, Mrs Banks makes me sound like my mother-in-law."

"Not a good thing?" Andy Quayle asked remembering a brief clash with the well known and notorious local lady politician, a woman known Island-wide for her firmly held and at times controversial opinions and her size twenty-two floral print suits.

"Er, no." Jemima smiled briefly, allowing him a glimpse of a happier, prettier and much younger woman.

"You say your husband phoned you this morning to let you know that he would be going out to lunch."

"Well, no, he phoned to say he might be but that he would ring to let me know for certain."

"And what time was this?"

"Oh about ten thirty this morning I think, no I remember now, it must have been a bit later than that, as Sandy called in at around a quarter to eleven to collect some books for a garage sale and Tony rang just as I was opening the door."

"And he didn't phone back?"

"No, which was odd, as normally he's good at that sort of thing. Only I have to know whether to eat with the children or with him later."

"I see. And did you phone him?"

"I tried to ring him on his mobile but it just rang and rang, so I called the receptionist and she said he'd left about eleven to meet a client for lunch."

"That's right officer, I've already checked with the member of staff concerned and it appears that Tony just walked out of the office and vanished off the face of the earth," Isla Fitzhammond advised, steepling her fingers and sinking further back into the large armchair from which a heady aroma of Chanel No 5 and alcohol emanated.

"And what happened to the client?"

"Well apparently after waiting for about fifteen minutes they rang the office as they couldn't reach Tony on his mobile and one of the junior advocates went down to the restaurant to smooth things over."

"And you rang Mrs Fitzhammond because?"

"Because I thought I'd ask her husband where my husband was as he – Tony – hadn't collected the children from swimming and he always does every Wednesday to save me the trip back into Douglas."

"Even when he's had lunch?"

"He takes a taxi."

"Any particular firm?"

"Telecabs mainly."

"Right, well, we'll check with them that they didn't pick him up at some point and with the other firms as well."

Andy cleared his throat – now for the awkward bit.

"Mr Banks wasn't in any way depressed when he left this morning?"

"No, not at all, he was quite the opposite as he was hoping for a bit of a dividend to go towards the holiday next weekend."

"And did he get it?"

"Good grief, I should say so; Alex signed a cheque to him for two-and-a-half grand this morning, or so Portia told me. So much for needing time to sort out my settlement because the firm is doing so badly, Men – they're all unmitigated bastards," Isla announced, and then on seeing the look passing between the two policemen hurriedly added, "Present company excepted of course."

PC Andy Quayle smiled frigidly and then addressed himself to Jemima who was watching Isla with embarrassed concern.

"A nice sum."

"I suppose so, yes, that's why he must have left the office early."

"Early?"

"Well he wasn't due at the restaurant until twelve and I wondered why he'd allowed so much time, he must have been going via the bank."

"Which one?"

"Royal Bank of Scotland," Jemima answered thoughtfully. "I can check with them to see if it went in."

"That would be a help, yes. Did he have any other accounts?"

"No."

Andy looked up; Isla had leant forward as if about to say something and then had sat back down.

"You were going to say something?"

"I …" Isla looked anxiously at Jemima and then muttered "I'm not sure whether I should say anything but Tony did have an account in the BVI."

"What!" Jemima exploded.

"He opened it about ten years back, something to do with his own personal pension fund," Isla explained.

"Oh." Jemima stared at her, her comfortable world was falling apart around her ears and her beloved husband, whom she had always considered a little too conservative and staid was fast achieving the reputation of one of spymaster John Le Carre's shadier characters.

There was a silence broken by the sudden strident ringing of the telephone. Isla gave Jemima a questioning look who in return wryly shrugged and nodded. Isla picked up the phone and after briefly clearing her throat announced in her best public school games mistress voice. "Banks residence, how may I be of assistance?" Isla listened carefully and then with a puzzled frown replaced the receiver and then fixed Jemima with a look which was suddenly almost but not quite sober.

"What did they want?" Jemima asked.

"What?"

"On the phone just then, only if it was Carol I'll have to call her back as I'm supposed to be doing the school run tomorrow."

"No it was ... was ..."

"It might be easier, madam, if you just told us and then we'll see whether or not it's important," Andy advised, watching her with undisguised interest.

"It was a voice – I don't know whose, sort of muffled and all it said was 'Get rid of them.'"

"Get rid of who?" Jemima asked.

"I have no idea, the police I guess," Isla remarked and then added "Cheese, I could do with a nice piece of cheese."

"And crackers," one of the children added staring at Isla in the same mesmerised way as both children had all evening, ever since she had arrived on their doorstep, bright red shoes in one hand and magnum of champagne in the other.

"Oh yes, can't have cheese without crackers," Isla replied, standing. She glared at both policemen and then clasping a child in each hand, lurched towards the lounge door. "You two might think about putting a tap on that," she added, nodding towards the telephone and then she abruptly left the room.

"Oh." Jemima, suddenly stricken, ran towards the large bay window and hastily closed the heavy linen curtains.

"I'm sure that it's nothing to worry about but we'll have that call checked anyway, and if you don't mind as your friend has suggested get a tap to your phone line. Is there anything else that your husband might have been hiding from you or that he was worried about?" Andy asked, realising with unhappy clarity born of experience that the missing man was becoming more difficult to find with each passing minute.

"No, I mean I didn't actually know about the account, I mean Tony was almost transparently honest," Jemima mused, her brows lowered in careful concentration.

"Did you have any sort of argument or anything before he left this morning? Or even last night?" Peter prompted.

"No, I can't think of anything ... he was a little preoccupied last night and very tired but I just assumed that he had a large case on this week and going into court always seems to drain him."

"So he seemed perfectly normal."

"Yes, he kissed me goodbye, said he'd pick up the kids from swimming and get them a McDonalds afterwards and asked me to buy some more dental floss."

"Dental floss." Andy looked up and met his fellow officer's look of concern. Men who were about to leave the family nest did not in his opinion worry about dental hygiene, even if they did have a secret account in the British Virgin Islands.

"Do you know if your husband had any enemies?"

"I don't know ... wait a minute there was a man who threatened him outside the court a month ago, said he had a few friends that Tony wouldn't want to meet and that they'd do anything for the price of a pint. Tony laughed it off until the man asked how his kids were doing at school and did little Tommy still like football?"

There was a brief silence while notes were made in identical notebooks.

"But it couldn't be him because he died about a week ago, heart attack or something," Jemima hurriedly added.

"Ah now that would have been our friend Mr Bonnington," Peter observed, making a careful note in a margin

"You know of him?"

"We have a file down at headquarters although not as large as the file at Manchester CID by all accounts. Dead or not we'll check a few of his associates, just in case. Anybody else Mrs Banks ... sorry, Jemima? Anyone you know of – clients, disgruntled employees?" Andy asked.

"Apart from Bonnington no one I can think of, Tony used to just do commercial work, banks mostly, contracts, trusts that sort of thing. Employees ... well there was a girl he got rid of but I hardly think ..."

"I'll have to ask her a few questions just in case."

"Portia may have her current address, I do know that after all the fuss the cheeky madam asked Tony for a reference, and needless to say he refused to give her one. There was that young chap that drank but he's in rehab at the moment in England and I hardly think ..."

"Even so, we'll have to check. Does Mr Banks own any other property or have another vehicle, that is apart from the one here and the one parked behind the office."

"We have a holiday house in Spain but it's let out at the moment for six months to a young couple who are in some sort of cabaret. I'll get you the address and their number."

Jemima got up and then stopped and turned towards them as a thought hit her. "You don't actually think that Tony is …" Jemima looked from one policeman to the other, noting that the frank and friendly smiles were becoming increasingly fixed.

"To be perfectly honest Mrs Banks, Jemima, we have no idea what to think," Andy admitted, looking again at his notes.

Jemima nodded and then left the room. Both policemen could hear the sounds of footsteps mounting the stairs and then after a short while their slow return. Jemima silently handed them a wad of documents. She looked tearful and the uneasy poise she had tried valiantly to hold on to was now clearly seen to be failing fast. Isla Fitzhammond who had followed her from the hall gave the two young men a questioning look and then asked if the children were still needed as she intended on feeding them and then they would all watch the Simpsons in the den. On being told that they weren't, she about-turned and rustled off towards the back of the house and the kitchen.

Jemima handed over a brown document wallet and then a passport and several sheaves of paper.

"That's the file with the Spanish details and this is his passport and this just came off the fax machine. It says that the bank in the BVI has just cleared his cheque for five hundred thousand pounds." There was a moment's stunned silence. Jemima, close to breaking down, cleared her throat before exclaiming, "I have no idea where the money has come from, especially as we were scraping around trying to find the money to pay the builder last week. But if he's got that amount and for some reason he's run away, why is his passport still here and why hasn't he taken the car?"

Andy's mobile rang and when answered made the puzzled expression on his face deepen. After he had finished a more than usually one-sided conversation he sat back and stared unseeingly at the floor.

"Well?" Jemima demanded.

"That was headquarters. My … er … Inspector says that no one fitting your husband's description or name has either left the Island by air, even privately, or gone on the ferry, as due to high winds this evening's boat was cancelled and the one that went this morning left before Mr Banks left the office. And …"

"Just please tell me," Jemima begged.

"A lady walking her dog on Douglas Beach has found a body washed up in a rock pool down near the old Summerland site and it appears to be wearing the sort of clothes that your husband may have been wearing."

"Oh." Jemima stared blankly at them.

"We don't get many bodies washing up on the tide but when they do they normally don't wear a pinstripe suit and gold cufflinks and it had one of those detachable court collars."

"Oh God, will I have to identify the body?"

"Yes, I'm afraid so."

Together they rose from their comfortable seats and walked towards the sounds of childish laughter and the overture to the Simpsons.

* * *

Some time later Jemima stared down at the inert and soggy lump of cloth and flesh that had once been a living breathing human being and with a shake of her head informed the waiting, silently staring police officers and coastguards that the body they had found was not the early remains of her husband Tony Banks, advocate, notary public and commissioner for oaths but that as far as she could tell it was wearing Tony's clothes and the cufflinks were definitely the ones she had herself given her husband that Christmas.

★ ★ ★

Sarah Corkill rushed headlong through the open door and slammed it shut behind her. "I'm so sorry I'm late …" she gasped, setting down two large dripping carrier bags onto the dusty wooden floor beside the chair that John Smith had thoughtfully shoved towards her.

"So which one of the children died this time?" Marianna Crowe asked.

"I … look I said I was sorry, all right and …"

"And she's here now," Stella Corlett interjected. "So can we please get on?"

"Fine, it's just that I can't start the scene without her as you all very well know. I wouldn't mind so much but I have visions of her stumbling onto the stage the first night, explaining that little Josh lost his PE kit again and her darling little Emmakins has raging lurgy and I really don't think that the paying audience will go 'Ah bless!'" Marianna railed as she stood up and paced across the empty space to take up her starting position.

"Don't take any notice of her, pet," Stella muttered soothingly as Sarah fumbled in one of the carrier bags for her script, "two of her many husbands left her before celebrating their first anniversary and the others drank themselves to death, and as for children I very much doubt that she's ever yet managed to eat a whole one."

Sarah giggled and hurried over to the back of the room.

She was in the process of carrying an imaginary tray into an imaginary lounge when Richard Allan arrived.

"Ah good, you've started," he barked, looking around. "Is Geoff here?"

"Making a cup of coffee," Eve mumbled, pointing in the vague direction of the church hall's diminutive kitchenette.

"Right, well in that case I'd like to start from Act One, Scene Two, beginning from Elvira's entrance."

"I thought we were doing Act One, Scene One?" Marianna hissed complainingly as she flicked through her script. "I thought that that was the entire point in having a bloody rehearsal schedule!"

"But I'm not sure I really know those lines yet," Geoff muttered, sipping a steaming mug.

"Then you'll be grateful for the extra time practising, won't you?" Richard stated, settling himself down in a central position in front of them.

"It's an awful lot to learn and I do have a job as well, you know," Geoff grumbled.

"I know it's a lot to take in Geoff, but as I said at the outset, the part of Charles requires a huge amount of hard work and dedication and at the time you promised me that you'd do anything to get the part, including taking a few days off work to learn your lines," Richard snapped back.

Marianna, who was valiantly trying to remember her new first cue as Ruth, walked over to Eve who was huddled over her highlighted and tatty script. Eve was beginning to question her desire to take on the part of Mrs Bradman, which since the auditions where they read the part straight from the book, had appeared to grow from a few witty one-liners to reams of incomprehensible words.

Richard settled himself further into his uncomfortable plastic chair and ignoring the gently muttering figure of Geoff Caine addressed the rest of the cast from the depths of his own heavily mutilated script.

"Elvira, you enter from the French windows, which we marked out yesterday and which the Brownies don't appear to have managed to fully rub out yet."

Frances Myers, realising that she was first on, hastily swallowed the remains of a bacon and egg sandwich and hurried over to the gently scuffed chalk marks. Richard, his head still buried in his scribbled notes, continued with his instructions. "Charles, you enter on the cue of 'Elementals' from the door at the back, but you don't see Elvira until after your next entrance and then you drop the glass, well the plastic beaker."

Richard then looked up, sat back and waited patiently and then as nothing had happened scowled at Marianna who was deep in conversation with Eve. Slowly realising that there was a silence, which only they were filling, both women stopped chatting and guiltily looked up. Finally they caught Richard's disapproving eye and with a start hastily tried to remember their opening lines.

" … I'm really very cross with him," Marianna haltingly announced as she took her place as Ruth

Frances, also realising with a jolt that she was now supposed to be on stage, moved furtively from the chalk mark to the far side of the room, via the other three actors now occupying various plastic chairs.

"Elvira, you need to float from one person to another, gracefully and somehow alluringly. I want the audience to see the stark contrast between wives, you the young, vibrant, feisty, high-maintenance first wife and Ruth the slightly dominating but kindly mother figure. At the moment Elvira, you have all the sexual charisma of a wet sponge and the grace of a particularly uncoordinated grave digger and Ruth is as likely to have attracted someone like Charles as I have of running the London Marathon."

"Oh!" Frances and Marianna gasped.

"So we will do it again from the beginning and this time ladies it would be nice if you could actually remember your characters and actually try to act for a change," Richard snapped.

The next attempt was slightly better, Marianna having remembered most of her lines, although frequently not in the correct order and Geoff the point at which he was supposed to first see Elvira and drop the glass.

After about an hour of fumbled lines Richard called for a break and tottered off, clutching two Ibruprofen capsules and a sachet of instant hot chocolate.

Marianna furtively extracted a packet of cigarettes from her commodious leather handbag and snuck outside, where she hid in the shelter of the porch and carefully lit herself a cigarette.

"Well, it's improving a bit," John remarked, joining her.

"And we only have, let me see, two weeks before the first curtain call?" Marianna offered the packet to John and then took a long drag of nicotine until the familiar heady feeling of warmth and wellbeing filled her brain, now almost completely jumbled with half-remembered lines and directions.

"To be honest, it's almost there," John puffed.

"Well it is for you, I'm on for almost the entire first half and as for Geoff I have absolutely no idea how he remembers all of his part."

"Photographic memory."

"Really?"

"He told me last night."

"Lucky sod."

"When do the costumes turn up?" John asked, leaning against the brick-lined wall.

"Richard said they would be here by Friday from that place in Liverpool, although we have to provide some of the tops and the shoes of course."

"It will be much better with the proper clothes."

"Yes I suppose so."

"So tell me just what it was that had you and my wife huddled in a corner for all intents and purposes like a pair of foul and midnight hags?"

"You haven't heard?"

"No that's why I'm asking you."

"Lou Sphinx is going to be filming that programme of his at the Gaiety the same week as we open."

"What!"

"Ah, I thought you'd be pleased."

"Have you any idea what that, that …" John spluttered, almost beside himself.

"Oh yes, I know all about the seance and the death of your mother, Eve told me."

"I suppose she also told you that after going to one of his private sessions she committed suicide."

"Eve said she'd convinced herself that your father wanted her to join him and she was in considerable pain."

"What about my pain?" John replied, viciously grinding the stub of his cigarette into the baked ground with his heel.

"And mine ..."

"Yours?"

"I was engaged to him once, many, many years ago."

"Oh, what happened?"

"I turned up at the church in a long white dress, heavy with child and accompanied by my entire family and most of our friends and the bastard caught a plane to Minorca with my maid of honour."

"I'm sorry I didn't know you had children."

"I don't. Lost it a few days later, stress, grief, hormones, who knows, stillborn – couldn't have any more." Marianna stared out into the gathering dusk as the last ribbons of light began to disappear behind the distant hills. Midges danced in and out of the fuchsia hedge shielding the church hall from the road, its branches laden with red and purple pendulous blooms, which were still gently dripping from an earlier shower of rain.

"I like fuchsia," Marianna observed, tossing her cigarette butt onto the front step and grinding it to a pulp with her foot.

"Really? I like nasturtiums myself," Geoff chuckled, materialising silently beside them.

"Where the hell have you been?" Marianna asked as he squeezed past her.

"Just out for a breath of fresh air," he replied with a broad wink before disappearing inside.

Marianna and John gave him a careful glance of knowing consideration and then followed him in. Sarah watched them return to the snug confines of the hall from her vantage point of damp leaves and re-buttoned her blouse.

Richard leant against one of the trestle tables, the set designs spread out in front of him and pointed to an area which might cause a few problems during the final scene. Harvey muttered a few soothing words and started drawing an alternative. A door banged shut and Richard looked up in time to see Sarah returning to her usual niche and her discarded script, there was a leaf caught up in a lock of damp hair which curled around the nape of her neck. Richard sighed he hoped that whatever dalliance she was currently occupied with would continue until at least the last night, the artistic temperament he could cope with but spurned lust he wasn't so sure about.

In a corner John dwelled on what Marianna had told him but decided for once not to share that knowledge with his more garrulous partner. Marianna watched him from her own corner and daydreamed of revenge, eaten cold and with a very large spoon.

Chapter Four

Mannanan glared down the full length of his substantial roman nose at the middle-aged and rather scrawny individual in front of him and counted to ten under his breath. It did absolutely no good at all.

"You are in fact dead," Mannanan stated, looking again at the list neatly pinned to his pristine clipboard.

"Dead?"

"Deceased, passed over, defunct, dead."

"Oh."

"Not breathing," added a voice from behind him.

Mannanan turned and stared frostily at the speaker.

"And what in God's name are you doing here?" Mannanan demanded testily.

Barty West just grinned and continued picking his teeth with a ghostly toothpick.

"But I can't be, you know … dead."

"Why not?"

"I'm not ready."

"Nobody ever is," Mannanan remarked, looking out to

sea. The matchstick figures he had been covertly observing began to finally move the black shiny body bag towards a waiting van, after which they slowly separated, a few returning to the distant glinting seashore to continue their search before the tide turned and obliterated the signs of any struggle that might have taken place. Although so far, to Mannanan's certain knowledge, nothing had been found apart from the scratchy marks of seabirds intent on an early dinner or late lunch and the clear footprints of the finders of the body, both two- and four-legged.

"Are you Death then?" the man asked.

"No," Mannanan answered.

"Right. Then … er … why are you here?"

"Because of the rules and regulations pertaining to and governing unnatural death."

"I thought there was something fishy about that bloke," the man sighed.

"The regulations clearly state that you are entitled to do one of three things. Firstly, you can go over to the other side having forgiven the person or persons who caused your death. Or secondly you can ask for someone to act on your behalf to bring about justice if they can. Or thirdly, you can refuse to leave the mortal plane until you yourself are satisfied that justice has been served. Justice, that is, in the moral rather than the legal sense."

"There's a difference?" the man asked.

"Oh yes." Mannanan muttered, "there most certainly is."

"Oh I don't know, really I don't, I mean I don't want to cause any trouble."

"Cause … Trouble …" Barty West exploded. "You've just been murdered – how much more trouble can you cause?"

"The thing is, I don't think he meant to do it."

"Who?"

"Mr Banks."

"Not Tony Banks?" Barty West spluttered.

"Yes."

"But Tony wouldn't hurt the proverbial fly, I mean he lets spiders out through the window, I've seen him do it."

"You know him?" Mannanan asked, frowning.

"Sure, he was articled to the advocate that set up all my companies, you know before ..." Barty stared at Mannanan who stared equally thoughtfully back and then they both stared at the man.

"So you are not actually Tony Banks then?" Mannanan asked, looking down at his list, which had the words *Anthony Lawrence Banks* clearly printed halfway down.

"Er no, I was just doing him a favour."

"Some favour," Barty muttered.

"Then who are you?" Mannanan asked, pointedly ignoring Barty West's constant interjections.

"Nigel Collins, I'm an estate agent."

"Well that explains everything," Barty scoffed.

"Barty, if you do not want to spend the next hundred years in a very small bottle I'd shut up now." Mannanan snapped as he flicked through his list. The name Nigel Collins appeared nowhere at all on any of the carefully typed pages.

"Somebody somewhere has perpetrated the administrative balls-up of the decade," he barked, reaching for the mobile phone in his jacket pocket. Nigel watched with interest as he flicked the cover open and searched for a number.

"Does it do pictures?" Nigel asked wistfully.

"I think so," Mannanan answered, pressing a button.

They all waited and then Mannanan on being connected to the right disembodied voice tersely explained the situation. There was a short silence punctuated by the single word 'Shit' and then another silence.

"I'll ring you back," the voice intoned after a while.

"Good, you do that," Mannanan remarked in carefully neutral tones, "and in the meantime what do I do with Nigel?"

Nigel shuffled his feet and thrust his hands in the pockets of his ill-fitting suit.

"I thought death would be a bit like the Vikings, you know lots of booze and birds in metal bikinis with leather skirts and enormous great big tits. Something to really snuggle into on a cold night," Nigel whined.

"Is that what you really want?" Mannanan asked in a much kinder tone.

"Oh yes."

"Right then, well as you died on the Isle of Man I see no reason why you can't have a proper Manx passing." Mannanan connected to another department and after re-explaining the situation and Nigel's request listened for a brief moment and then disconnected with a beaming smile.

"Nigel, you are going to get one humdinger of a celestial party."

"Really?"

"Oh yes."

"When?"

Mannanan looked skywards and then chuckled happily. "About now, I'd say," he answered.

A large blonde woman sporting a leather helmet, a tiny polished silver and leather uplift bra and a very short skirt of soft pleated suede, suddenly appeared in front of them accompanied by a loud popping sound.

"Nigel Collins?" she asked.

"Here," Nigel answered, tentatively raising his hand.

The woman advanced purposely towards him, her breasts straining against the leather like two sun-ripened Ogen melons floating in a very small pool. Nigel swallowed and looked her straight in the cleavage.

"You do not look like a warrior, no?" she bellowed, standing in front of him, her leather booted feet comfortably astride and her hands placed firmly on large and curvaceous hips.

Nigel swallowed again and then dribbled.

"Er, no."

"Here." A sheep's horn was thrust at him and Nigel, looking down into the open bone, sighed.

"Mead," he whimpered and then drank a long and sustaining draft.

"Ah, you can drink," the woman observed, mildly impressed as he completely drained the drinking vessel and wiped his lips with his sleeve.

"Perhaps you can also do other things?" she smiled salaciously at him and then, scooping him up and hauling him over one shoulder, turned and carried him off and up towards the mackerel slatted sky.

"I thought they always came on a horse?" Barty remarked.

"No, not always, it's the saddle, dammed uncomfortable, always gets in the way."

"What?" Barty smirked, getting the joke just as he realised that Mannanan was no longer there.

"Hang about, wait for me ..." he cried, disappearing into the soft embrace of a passing breeze.

* * *

Tony Banks merged with the crowd watching the searchers on the beach and turned in a thoughtful fashion towards the ferry terminal. "The night boat leaves in an hour's time and by the time they had identified the body I will," he reasoned, "be safely sitting in Liverpool Airport waiting for the first flight out to the Canaries. Jemima will be all right and so will the children, it will all be all right. It would, it had to be."

He was still trying to think of some way of letting his nearest and dearest know that he was still in the land of the living when he spotted the first policeman. The young constable stood woodenly just outside the ferry terminal entrance and was earnestly checking the faces of people going in against whatever information he had printed on the sheet of paper clutched in one hand.

Tony stopped and bent down to tie the laces on his trainers and took a surreptitious look around. The place seemed to be crawling with coppers and they all had the same piece of paper on them and he'd have bet even money on the fact that what the paper contained was a recent picture of him. Tony straightened up and moved away towards the promenade wall at exactly the same time as Bob Callow emerged from the side entrance of the terminal building.

Swearing profusely under his breath, Tony turned his back on the waiting ferry and walked back down the promenade. He had nowhere to go and about a thousand pounds in cash, he couldn't stay in a hotel or even a local guesthouse, as somebody somewhere would recognise him, someone always did and he couldn't sleep rough because he had no idea how to.

He was standing by the old garages opposite the stage door of the Gaiety Theatre, some time later, when the mad idea first hit him. He'd been there often enough and the place was a warren, you could hide in there for days and no one would even suspect, it would be warm and there were facilities of sorts.

The back door was wide open as a few able-bodied men were attempting to manhandle large expanses of hardboard and Victorian-style furniture into a waiting van. Tony ambled across the road and when the men were safely inside the van with their backs turned away from him, he moved quickly past the railings, through the gaping entrance and taking a sharp left tiptoed down past the dressing rooms. He vaguely remembered that there was a doorway, somewhere along the dimly lit corridor, that would eventually lead to another corridor connecting the backstage area to the main theatre. And he was fairly certain that somewhere along that route there would be places to hide until he could make it down to the basement.

An hour later he huddled in the dark under the wooden stage and realised exactly what he had done. Tears trickled slowly down his face as he gulped back a sob at the exact same time as something furry scuttled across his foot.

He screamed.

The blackness of the total absence of light settled like a heavy cloak around his shoulders and his stomach groaned in protest.

"When was the last time you had anything to eat, lad?" a voice barked from the space directly in front of him.

"What?" Tony managed to squeak, desperately trying to see the speaker.

"Food, sustenance, you know, meals like?"

"Er, I had a bowl of cereal at breakfast."

"Cardboard confetti in a box," the speaker muttered, "that's not proper nosh."

"No."

"No, what you need to start the day is a big sustaining bowl of porridge made with real oats mind, not the pap in a bag they pass off as oats …"

"Brown sugar …" Tony agreed with a sigh, his stomach rumbling again in protest.

"Aye lad, and a plate of sausages with a hunk of warm bread and at least two eggs, runny and yellow."

"With a big mug of tea," Tony nodded, fear overcome by hunger so real it actually hurt.

"Or kippers with lime marmalade and brown bread and butter …"

"Marmalade?"

"Aye, traditional that is, cuts the smokiness of the fish, nothing like a good Manx kipper." There was a slight pause and then someone sat down next to him. The unmistakable aroma of pipe tobacco floated in the air and Tony sniffed appreciatively.

"So if it's not too personal a question, what the 'ell are you doing down here in the dark with me?" the voice asked, between alternating puffs on an invisible pipe.

"I've run away and I might have killed a man."

"Might? You mean you don't know whether or not he's dead?"

"No, he's dead all right I saw it happen."

"Then you must know whether you killed him, I mean it's not the sort of thing that you wouldn't notice, like?"

"It's a bit complicated."

"Well begin at the start and carry on until you get here,

I like a bit of a story now and then, breaks the monotony, see."

"Oh."

"Well ..."

"It all started with a phone call from one of my clients, he says he ..."

"What?"

"He said that I had a very pretty wife and two adorable children and wouldn't it be a shame if they had a little accident."

"How little?"

"I didn't ask – it was enough just to know that he knew them."

"And did he – know them, that is?"

"He told me where they went to school and he described my wife shopping in Tesco's, he even told me what she was buying and then another voice came on the line and described my kids playing in the playground and I could hear them, you know, shouting and running about."

"What sort of an accident?"

"They didn't say, they just laughed."

"Oh."

"They laughed a lot."

"Right."

"I asked them what they wanted and they said I was to walk out of the office at eleven thirty and meet them in the St Georges wine bar, in the meantime I would find something in that morning's post."

"And did you?"

"Yes."

"What?"

"A plain brown envelope stuffed with used twenty pound

notes, fifteen hundred pounds of soiled twenty pound notes and a note saying 'get lost'. Well, I just panicked, walked out of the office clutching the envelope and my briefcase and just kept on walking until I got to St Georges churchyard where I bumped into one of the down and outs. I knew him vaguely years ago, he used to be an estate agent before his wife left him and he turned to the inside of any bottle that would stop him from sobering up. I asked him if he'd swap clothes with me and after he'd stopped laughing and realised that I was serious he agreed. I gave him some money, enough to keep him happily drunk for at least a month and we changed in the toilets inside the church. He left and I hung around in the porch for a bit and then when I came out I saw, saw ..." Tony stopped his mouth dry as he remembered what had happened next.

"What?"

"Two men – they had him between them and they were sort of carrying him along the path towards the gate that connects the church yard to Hope Street. And I think he was dead, he had this gash on the side of his head and his neck was held really oddly, can't describe it that well but I sort of knew."

"Perhaps he was just knocked out?"

"Perhaps."

"You don't sound all that certain."

"Anyway, I stuffed the rest of the money in a plastic carrier I found in the church porch and then I went down to the promenade, spent all day just wandering around the rocks below Summerland and just when I'd got up enough courage to go back, this body falls right past me from the road above ... and it's him, wearing my clothes with blood all over the collar of my best striped shirt and with his head bashed in. Well – I tell you this for free – I really panicked then, ran along the side of the cliffs half demented until I saw some woman with a dog and legged it back towards the prom."

"And did anyone see you."

"You know, that was the oddest thing, wearing the tramp's clothes, it was like I was a non-person, like I was just invisible; I mean people went to huge lengths not to look at me, not to notice, to sort of will me gone. I guess that's what it's like all the time for those poor beggars, and you know, I do the same thing every day myself when I see one."

"Humm."

"Anyway, I waited for someone to find the body, which the lady with the dog did eventually and I hung around while the police came and I watched my, my wife ... go down to identify it and then I tried to get on the night boat."

"Right."

"I'd changed you see, bought some jeans and a sweatshirt from one of those shops along the front, didn't think of eating, couldn't concentrate. And then I saw them, the two men watching the police, hanging around just like me. It was surreal, like one of those old-fashioned silent films. They left after the police had gone and then I left too, only the cops must have had photos of me before they found the body, because they were waiting for me outside the ferry terminal and I recognised one of them and he ... well he would have recognised me too. And then I spotted them striking the set here and thought why not hide in the space under the stage for a bit."

"And you don't know why this bloke that rang you wanted you to go away?"

"No idea at all."

"Must have had some reason. Who was this client of yours anyway?"

"Bartholomew West."

"West … West … rings a bit of a nasty bell that, have no idea why, but it will come lad, it will come. Any idea why this character wanted you off the Island and a million miles away?"

"No idea at all, I mean he's not the nicest guy in the world but I wouldn't have thought that he'd kill me. I mean, why?"

"And you do what for him?"

"I deal with his companies, set up business deals, draft contracts, company minutes, that sort of thing, nothing dodgy as far as I know."

"Curiouser and curiouser."

"Yes."

"Still, first things first, what you need is something to eat and drink. Stay there a tick, I won't be long."

"But …" Tony strained into the darkness and felt rather than saw his companion leave. About ten minutes later something landed in the darkness at his feet, and scrabbling around he found a crumpled plastic bag containing a packet of crisps, packets of nuts both dry roasted and ready salted, a box of matches, two cans of coke and a selection of chocolate.

"Sorry it's only cold stuff lad … but I can't get you a hot drink until the manager opens up in the morning," Tony's new-found friend advised between puffs as he tried to relight his pipe.

Tony opened the crisps and one of the cans by touch and began to eat voraciously; never had junk food tasted so good.

"Thanks, er ... by the way what is your name?"

"Harry."

"Thanks Harry, I owe you."

"That's all right lad, I like the company, don't get much down here."

"So Harry, what do you do?"

"Do? Well, not a lot really. I suppose you could say that I look after the security side of things."

Tony trembled. "Security?"

"Oh don't worry lad, you're safe enough down here. And I wouldn't tell a soul."

"Promise?"

"Promise."

"Cross your heart and hope to die," Tony whispered, remembering the chant he'd often made as a child.

"No, I can't promise that."

"Why not?" Tony hissed desperately.

"Technically impossible, being as I'm already dead."

Tony stopped in mid-crunch and, with trembling fingers, found, fumbled and eventually lit a match. Light blazed around the wooden structures above and around his head.

Suddenly it was blown out and a voice from right in front of him stated "Don't do that lad, all this wood, naked flame, use your loaf, boy."

"Harry?"

"Yes?"

"Won't do it again."

"Good; them matches is for emergencies and so's you can find the toilet, tomorrow I'll nick a torch and get you some proper food."

"Thanks."

"No bother really, and now I'll find you some sort of bedding, there's always something left behind after a play."

"Why are you doing this?" Tony asked the darkness straight ahead of him.

"Dunno really," Harry replied, his voice moving off into the distance. "Perhaps it's just because I haven't had a pet for a while now, not one that talked anyway."

And with that he was gone.

* * *

Bartholomew West scowled down at the invoice in his hand and then violently tore it in half and then half again. If they thought that for one minute he was actually going to pay to keep his own companies going, they were in for one very nasty big fat shock.

"Laura," he shouted, "get me Mr Haslett on the phone – and do it now."

There was a muttered "Yes, Mr West" from a distant unseen corner and then the phone beside him rang.

"Haslett, West. That matter we discussed, has it been finalised?"

West waited as the voice on the other end spoke at length. Finally he put the phone down and then abruptly collapsed into the soft leather of his executive swivel chair, his face, for all of its artificial tan, suddenly pale.

"Shit!" he exclaimed, wiping a bead of sweat from his forehead.

He'd told the buggers to persuade Tony to disappear, not knock him over the head and then throw him off a cliff and now it seemed that they hadn't even got that right. Well, it all boiled down to the one golden rule he'd stuck to through thick and thin, if you want to do something right then do it yourself. He'd got lazy, fat and idle and it was time to sort things out. Personally.

Chapter Five

Bob Callow sat back in his comfortable seat, surveyed the vast golden expanse of Douglas Bay sparkling in the late afternoon sunshine with something akin to national pride and took a tentative sip of coffee. It wasn't as good as the stuff he'd had in Turkey but it wasn't bad. Greg Mathews watched him and then, turning to his companion, asked, "So Clive, have you met the old man yet?"

Bob spluttered into his cup and Clive looked from one to the other in frank astonishment.

"What old man?"

"Ah, so he hasn't introduced the two of you yet?"

Greg grinned down into his coffee cup and then with an evil twinkle in his eye stared at Bob until the latter turned a bright scarlet.

"What old man?" Clive reiterated.

"Mannanan Mac Lir," Greg whispered, "the ancient guardian of Mann, keeper of the faith, protector of the weak …"

"Have you been drinking?" Clive asked, giving Greg's coffee cup a suspicious look.

"No. But you might want to imbibe when you've heard about him," Greg answered, settling back into the soft and body-hugging contours of the sofa.

"Mannanan is a myth, the kids do it at school when they learn about our Celtic ancestors and produce their first Hop-tu-naa turnip lantern," Clive asserted, remembering the last elderly weathered vegetable root he'd attempted to carve for his youngest with an assortment of power tools.

"Blunted my best bit with that ruddy turnip; God knows how the blessed sheep actually eat them," he grumbled, remembering.

"Hop tu what?" Greg asked.

"Halloween to you lot across," Clive advised, pouring himself another coffee from the nearly drained cafetière.

"Well, legend or not, Bob can actually really see and speak to him," Greg snapped. "Gave me the willies the first time it happened, wasn't so bad the second time, I mean at least I didn't actually see anyone die."

"This substance abuse of yours, ever thought of getting professional help?" Clive hissed.

"All right, cut it out the pair of you. Clive … Greg, just shut up for a minute …" Bob wiped another bead of moisture from his forehead with an off-white cotton handkerchief and took a deep breath. "I wasn't going to say anything because after we nailed that mad writer …"

"The one who thought he was a two-thousand-year-old serial rapist, with cannibalistic tendencies?"

"Couple of years ago, yes."

"You and Brian Clague rearranged the Cliffs down near the Chasms?"

"Yes."

"And this Mannanan character helped you sort it out?"

"Yes."

"Any chance he got rid of the Mad Druid as well?"

"Er yes, why?" Bob asked, frowning.

"No reason really, but a lot of rumours were flying around at the time and what with one thing and another, certain people reckoned that you'd been dabbling with the occult."

"What!" Bob exploded.

"Mind you, if it was just talking to dead people that's all right." Clive smiled beatifically at both Bob and Greg and took another custard cream from the plate in front of him.

"You mean you don't mind?" Greg asked.

"Nope. Doesn't bother me. My Aunt Aelish used to regularly speak to the dead, had the crystal ball, scented candles, the lot, mind you she used to think she was a lamp-post but then nobody's perfect, eh?"

"But Bob can really see him," Greg earnestly exclaimed, leaning over towards him.

"Doesn't that bother you at all?"

"No. Frankly the only thing that bothers me is that he didn't say anything about it himself. Well, Bob?"

"I would have said something if the old man had still been around but I hadn't heard anything since the Glashton episode, well not until today."

"And what's so special about today?"

"He came back."

"And this just slipped your mind?" Clive sniffed in a mildly offended fashion.

"Well yes, I mean he's been downgraded and well …"

"But can he still get into rooms without being seen, open locked drawers, eavesdrop without the usual devices?"

"Well I suppose so … yes."

"Good. Does he subcontract?"

"I could ask ..." Bob muttered uncertainly.

"Only he might be cheaper than the usual electronic equipment and our start-up costs are high enough as it is," Clive rumbled.

"Right. So you don't mind?"

"No, not really, after all he might come in really useful, especially if we're working to protect a ghost hunter like Lou Sphinx."

"Couldn't you just do the world a favour and not protect him?" Greg remarked acidly.

"And lose our first commission?" Bob sniffed. "I don't think so."

"Besides, what have you got against him? I thought you'd only met him once," Clive asked.

"Once was enough, believe me, once is all anybody ever needs," Greg replied, wincing at the memory.

"So now that this Mannanan character is back, is he willing to help out a private enterprise such as our good selves?" Clive enquired, dunking another biscuit in his cooling coffee.

"Well yes, although it's a bit of a quid pro quo situation," Bob muttered.

"Oh?"

"He wants us to do a bit of digging on some bloke named Bartholomew West."

"Oh, and what does he want to know about that particular greasy little slime ball?" Greg snapped.

"You know him?"

"Oh yes, I know him all right, the vicious, corrupt little ... I mean to say, who doesn't?"

"Hold on a minute Greg, you do mean now?"

"Well yes, of course I mean now, he runs some mega-rich property development company, all above board except that as he's running it there has got to be some scam going."

"This is runs … present tense?"

"Yes. Why?"

"Well, the Bartholomew West I want to know about was murdered thirty-odd years ago in the cellar of one of the old Victorian hotels at the back of Douglas Prom."

"Murdered!" Greg exclaimed.

"Aye and by person or persons unknown, which is why I've been asked to help find the killer or killers."

"I know that I'm really going to regret asking this, but why?"

"Because the body has just come to light and old Barty West wants closure or …"

"Or?"

"He's apparently going to singlehandedly shorten an already short tourist season."

"And your old mate is involved in this because?"

"Because he's lost his Minor Deity status and is now working as a member of some obscure government department under tourism and when I say under, I mean physically, in the basement."

"All very surreal. Although considering the dead weights currently running things hardly surprising," Clive chuckled.

"There can't be two Bartholomew Wests, can there?" Greg muttered thoughtfully.

"And that's exactly what I intend to find out," Bob barked as he bit into a crumbly wedge of shortcake.

* * *

Bartholomew West the living surveyed the vast expanse of sea outside the large picture window of his office with a jaundiced air; he'd always held the opinion that the sea was a complete waste of good building land but even he had to admit that even a glimpse of it from the top of a toilet cistern could pay dividends price-wise.

The plasma screen on the wall next to him flickered as someone shot someone else and then dived off the edge of a submarine.

The telephone rang unanswered as Bartholomew West returned to his now uncluttered desk and picked up his private phone, the one that had its own line and didn't need to go through his secretary first.

He waited for Haslett to answer and drummed his fingers impatiently against the polished surface of his desk.

"Well?" he barked. "Does she know where the little sod has disappeared to?"

He listened and then gave a long drawn out sigh of frustration.

"Well, if she doesn't know anything she doesn't. Did you find that hacker?"

This time the proffered answer made him smile, his features creasing into rolls of fleshy mirth.

"Good, good, pay him in cash and then tell him I need another little job done; no better yet, tell him I need to verify the results, give him half and then let him know that he will get the rest when we meet up ... yes I thought the boat would do nicely as well."

He hung up, pleased at the prospect that at least something had gone right, and was in quite a good mood when his mobile phone rang.

"West here .... Oh, it's you Daryl ... And why would I

do that? Meet you where? ... Yes I know that someone is asking questions about the body ... but ... no you hang on ... I don't have that amount of cash to hand ... I'll meet you there then ... well where? ... Oh for goodness sake, Daryl, give me a little time ... Where are you working at the moment? The Gaiety Theatre? ... I'll see you there somewhere secluded ... The boiler room? Perfect, perfect ... and I'll bring the money..."

He sat and in a fit of sudden temper pulled the phone socket from the wall and hurled his mobile phone across the room and then as if that action had proved cathartic stared unseeingly across the room.

"Thinks that I don't do my own dirty work, does he? Well, if you want something done you have to do it yourself and no, Mr Daryl-shit-for-brains-Smith, the only payment you will get tonight will be a small gold coin to pay the ferryman with."

* * *

Richard regarded the elderly carpenter in front of him and tried not to look at the wart, or at least not too obviously.

"But we put all the stuff there," he reiterated.

"Well, I haven't moved it," the old man barked back.

"But nobody else is here," Richard remarked, looking around the empty space at the back of the stage. Without the completed set and without the canvas backdrop, the cold and musty air seemed to loom almost malevolently over the heads of the last two people left alone in the empty theatre.

A door banged shut and, startled, they both turned towards the sound. Footsteps marched purposely towards them, followed by the clicking of sharpened nails meeting a rough concrete floor. A man emerged from the top of the stairs leading down from the back door and stopped to glare at them both. The large dog beside him abruptly sat on his haunches and snuffled at the damp air.

"Who the hell are you?" Richard demanded of the blue uniformed stranger.

"I'm Security and this is Mike," the stranger answered.

Mike the Alsatian barked on cue and then regarded Richard with unblinking luminous brown eyes.

"Security?" George asked in a quavering voice, from behind Richards's large and well fed bulk.

"Aye, I'm to check this place out before Mr Sphinx arrives."

"Who?"

"Mr Sphinx, you know … off the TV."

"No, I don't know," Richard grumbled, glaring belligerently up at him.

The dog growled.

"I don't watch a lot of television, got better things to do with my time," Richard added, ignoring the dog who was now gently drooling.

"Well anyway, I haven't got time to stand around chatting all night …"

"And we have?" Richard interrupted, now thoroughly annoyed. "Our theatre group has paid to hire this place and nowhere in the contract or during the pre-production meetings did anyone inform us about your Mr Sphinx or for that matter that animal."

Mike glared at him and yawned.

"Well, all I know is that I have to secure the premises," the guard snapped, descending to their level.

"I don't suppose you've come across a pile of blankets

and a box of props in your travels?" George asked, backing away from Mike who was now avidly trying to sniff his shoes.

"No, but then I wouldn't be looking for blankets, would I?" The guard answered, as he marched off towards the door that separated the stage from the auditorium, Mike trotting happily in his wake, his wet nose picking up all sorts of weird and wonderful scents.

Richard was still looking for the missing items when he heard the howl and just about managed to leap clear as Mike raced past him, head down and hackles raised. George stopped hammering as the guard staggered to a halt beside him.

"What happened?" Richard and George asked in interested union.

"He's gone mad." The guard panted. "One minute he's sniffing one of them little rooms ... and the next he's jumped clean out and over the ledge and is scrambling about in the seats below me."

"Which, er, little room?" George asked.

"The one that had the curtains drawn."

"Ah, you mean that little room, which us as is used to the ways of the theatre call a box," George advised.

"Box, room ... booth ... what's the difference?"

"Well if it was that particular box, the one with the closed curtains, he must have seen the ghost," George remarked in hushed tones, sagely regarding the end of his hammer as if for some form of divine inspiration.

"Ghost?" the guard queried, looking nervously around him.

"Oh aye, he sits up there in one of them boxes, and he watches everyone, sometimes he flits around dressed up in his smart togs and if you is unlucky enough to see him … well …"

Richard, who had been avidly listening on the other side of the flat they were trying to fix, grinned.

"Well?" the guard asked, nervously moistening his lips with his tongue.

"Let's just say it's not a good thing, especially if you have a dicky ticker."

"You mean …"

"He frightens the unsuspecting soul into an early grave, I've known cleaners go stark staring mad, so I 'ave."

"Right, I don't suppose you saw where Mike went?"

"Should think he's halfway to Peel by now, or cowering by the back door," George replied after a moment's consideration.

"Thanks," the guard mumbled and then left in the direction of the stage door at a run.

"That wasn't very nice," Richard chuckled from his side of the canvas and wood panel.

"Well that bloody dog ate my tea," George grumbled unrepentantly, "and it was sausage and ketchup with extra sausage."

* * *

Jemima looked at the scrawled note in her hand and pushed a straying lock of hair behind her right ear. The paper, torn from the side of a brown paper bag, still had a globule of ketchup on the edge and the writing looked very much like eyeliner.

Dearest Gem,
I'm ok a friend is looking out for me.

They will hurt you if they think you know where I am
Love T

Brian Clague watched her brush away a tear before handing the paper to him.

"And this is definitely from your husband, Tony Banks?" he asked, handling the remnant of paper with care.

"Oh yes, that's Tony's writing, I'd know his scrawl anywhere, sometimes it gets so bad that he leaves me notes which even he can't read when he gets home. Thank God for Dictaphones and word processors," Jemima muttered, almost smiling.

"And this came when?" Brian asked.

"This morning. I rang as soon as it arrived and I'd opened it. At least he's OK and he's alive."

"And under a certain amount of fear and duress by the look of it I wonder where he got the … does that look like make-up to you?"

"Black eyeliner, although, well, it seems greasier … perhaps it's just cheap eyeliner."

"Does he have a female friend he's, er, close to?"

"If that is your polite way of asking if Tony has a mistress, the answer is no; what with work and the Rotary club and his family he wouldn't have the time."

"Or the energy," Brian grumbled almost to himself.

"Do you have children, Inspector?"

"Yes, two and the youngest is still producing nuclear waste from one end and indescribable stuff from the other, so yes I do know what you mean."

"I suppose you will have it looked at?"

"Oh yes, I'll do that all right … although I'm not sure it will do any good. Do you have the envelope?"

"I think so; I usually just throw them straight in the bin with the other stuff I don't open." Jemima disappeared from view and then returned moments later with a crumpled off-white envelope. Brian inspected it with something bordering on interest.

"This looks like it's been used more than once, including the stamp."

"It was – I had to pay the postman extra when he turned up."

"Curiouser and curiouser."

"Do you really think that Tony is … well … safe?"

"Oh yes … after all he's eating if the ketchup is anything to go by and somehow he managed to get to a post box, but …"

"What?"

"He may be being watched, or he could fear that he is otherwise why didn't he just ring? Writing this, pinching the envelope … it would have taken time and trouble which I'm afraid is what your husband through possibly no fault of his own is in a lot of."

"Poor Tony."

"Yes, poor Tony indeed."

Chapter Six

Nestling deep in a shady valley the world famous Fairy Bridge straddles the main road between the Island's capital of Douglas and the international airport. Above the bridge the Island's traffic roars, whilst underneath the fairy folk are purported to meet every second Wednesday where they happily whip up hexes against the Department of Transport and mobile-home owners. Tourists and locals in tune with their spiritual side often stop at this dappled historical site to ask for help and guidance, normally by either throwing a coin into the stream below or by committing their problem in writing to a varied selection of materials, including the ends of cereal packets, brand new England shirts and beer mats, and then attaching them by a variety of means, some more ingenious than others, to the limbs of the trees overlooking the tarmacked span.

Bob Callow leant against the white painted stone wall and gazed up at the tree above his head. Each and every branch appeared to have grown paper fruit in a variety of colours.

"These fairies you were muttering about, they don't actually read all of these, do they?" the youth with the acne, weak handshake and designer sunglasses asked in an interested voice.

Bob looked down at his companion and sighed. Dealing with Dynamic Dave from his employer's publicity department was like dealing with a fledgling police constable, fresh out of training and so wet behind the ears that he had difficulty in not patting him on the head and sending him down to the bakers with an order for doughnut ring holes.

"No, not all of them," Clive carefully answered, his voice muffled by the handkerchief he was trying not to suffocate himself with.

"Oh." Dave nodded to himself and ticked a box on the clipboard-held piece of paper he was studying.

"Any emanations?"

"Any what?" Bob asked, replacing the letter he had been reading from a poet in Doncaster, who was having problems with his virility and spelling.

"Emanations, you know, supernatural happenings?" Dave explained patiently, the mottled sunlight dancing on his blackened lenses.

"Well no, not really, apart that is from the odd wheel falling off and engine failure."

"Purely coincidental as it happens," Clive snorted.

"Although ..." Bob whispered in a hesitant fashion.

"Yes ..." Dave breathed, pen poised in mid-scribble.

"There have been sightings of the wee folk during Children in Need week."

"And when the local hospice needed a lot of money for a new building," Clive added helpfully.

"Right ... so nothing really."

"Well nothing that wasn't pink, fluffy, carrying a large plastic bucket and wearing a tutu," Bob answered as a car rushed past, eager to overtake the tipper truck in front.

"Manx fairies are more sort of Shakespearean …" Clive advised from the comfort of his wheelchair.

"Shakespearean?" Dave questioned his brow furrowing with the concentration of someone who normally found the *Daily Mail* a little too highbrow.

"Now there was a bloke who knew his fairy folk," Bob agreed, whilst reading the retired ramblings of a flight attendant from Hull.

"So what you are trying to tell me is that Manx fairies are not … er … nice?" Dave finally concluded after much slow and ponderous thought.

"Steal the milk out of a cow given half a chance," Clive affirmed.

"Swap your firstborn for a turnip …" Bob agreed.

"Aye and some mothers never even noticed, I mean you only have to look at the honourable members of the House of Keys and let's not even consider the Legislative Council," Clive grinned.

"Oh yes indeedy, much better not to consider them, I mean, nobody else does," Bob added with a mischievous twinkle in his eyes.

"That's like … your Government, isn't it?" Dave asked, whilst studiously writing it all down in careful longhand.

"Aye, transparent government is what we call it," Clive nodded sagaciously.

"Why?"

"Because you know the buggers must be doing something but no one has actually ever seen 'em doing it!" Clive scoffed.

"Right."

"Anyway that's the Fairy Bridge inspected, although I seriously doubt if the Department of Transport nannies will allow you to film here, on account of the accidents that might happen as motorists slow down to see what that bird who co-presents is almost wearing," Bob grunted, replacing the letters he'd been perusing.

"Although if they thought drivers might slow down to have a look ..." Clive mused, "... they might let you film."

"Now there's a thought, nubile young totty as traffic calmers. I can just see it now, instead of those sleeping policemen we'd have life-size models of Jordan standing at the side of the road with the number three on one boob and a nought on the other," Bob tittered.

"You can snigger, mate, but I can feel a letter to the editor coming on as we speak," Clive replied, a trifle sniffily.

"So you think that maybe we ought to just stick to the other sights?" Dave asked, looking from one to the other of his current mentors and then at the shadowed trees and the brightly whitewashed stone bridge they were leaning against.

"Might make things easier, anyway I thought that you just wanted to film in the Gaiety Theatre? Which by the way is going to be a big enough headache security-wise as it is, without having to also protect your principal out in the open. I mean to say, take a look at this place, sniper cover from every direction including the road. And to be honest with you lad, the evil-minded little buggers aren't exactly known for their co-operation," Bob earnestly advised him.

"So you really don't think that the little people would show?" Dave asked with a certain amount of disappointment.

"Er, no," Clive answered, turning his wheelchair back towards his parked van. "And if I were you, young David, I wouldn't call them little people either, especially not here," he added.

"Or wee folk – calling them that is almost as bad," Bob sighed and draped a long arm over the youth's shoulder in a fatherly fashion.

"Best if we just stick to the Gaiety, eh?" he rumbled. "Lots of guaranteed emanations there by all accounts, and more importantly we can ensure that your star presenter has at least a chance of avoiding the assassin's bullet."

"Well I …"

"What?"

"Oh, nothing …"

"Come on lad, spit it out …"

"Well, it's just that I'm not all that sure about it being a bullet. I mean it would be too quick for a start and if anyone was really out to get Mr Sphinx surely they would want it to be far more painful and long drawn out?"

"This Lou Sphinx isn't all that popular then?"

"Put it this way, if I knew who it was that wrote those letters I'd hold a whip-round to help pay for the ammunition."

"Ah."

"That's if it is on the level."

"But what about the cleaner?"

"If Mr Sphinx thought he'd get a bit more publicity and media coverage, especially with his new book about to be launched, he'd have added the crushed glass himself and cut his own brakeline."

"Really?"

"Oh yes. Frankly, I wouldn't put anything past him in his search for fame and fortune; even dying he'd keep death waiting whilst he signed autographs."

"So not Mr Popular?"

"No."

They stood in silence under the fluttering branches until a double-decker bus raced past grinding its gears and roaring like an incontinent and bad-tempered Tyrannosaurus with toothache. A stream of cars trailing in its wake passed both watchers by mere inches and hurtled up the road leaving Dave and Bob feeling dirty and semi-asphyxiated.

"Think we ought to be getting back to Douglas," Bob wheezed.

"Oh yes, let's," Dave agreed, coughing loudly. "By the way," he added as they walked quickly towards the waiting van, "anything interesting in those letters?"

"Nothing that a degree in Psychology and an Ann Summers' catalogue wouldn't cure." Bob replied, leading him back towards their hired vehicle and patiently waiting driver.

* * *

Russell Gillings-Cooper glared at his assistant stage manager with all the pent-up emotion left over from a previous meeting with his younger and more sartorial counterpart at the Villa Marina.

"Just run it past me again?" Russell patiently asked in carefully flat tones.

"George said ..."

"So you didn't see anything yourself?"

"Well no, not then ..."

"When?"

"I was checking the orchestra pit afterwards because young Sam said that she thought she'd seen a mouse and he was there crouched in the corner …"

"Who was?"

"The Phantom."

"The …. Oh come now, you surely don't expect me to believe that some nut is running around my theatre in an opera cloak and wearing a white mask?"

"George said he'd put down a packet of sandwiches and when he turned back from making a cup of coffee they'd gone."

"Perhaps they fell down the back of something?"

"He looked, it was the first thing he did …"

"And the second thing …"

"He discovered the coffee had gone."

"A ghost that eats and drinks?"

"Well, er, yes …"

"The other alternative is that one of the morons currently employed in sorting out the toilet plumbing forgot to bring their own lunch so pinched George's?"

"I, well, er …"

"And has anybody else seen this masked man?"

"Doris thought she saw someone in one of the boxes when she was cleaning the carpets this morning."

"But she wasn't sure?"

"Er …"

"Doris is never sure. Ever since that woman discovered satellite and interactive psychic television, she's been seeing hooded cloaked figures everywhere, including the biscuit aisle at Shoprite, so I'd take everything she says with a very large pinch of salt. Now get out, buy George another round of sandwiches and for goodness sake clear the backstage area – we have that private detective arriving some time today and the last thing we need is some mad intruder who likes dressing up and pretending to be the Lone Ranger without either a horse or Tonto."

"Actually he was more Lloyd Webber than Antonio Banderas ..."

"Really? And this is of interest to me because ..."

"I'll go buy George another sandwich."

Russell watched as the youth sidled out, and after the door of his office had finally closed reached into one of the lower drawers of his desk. His hands searched for the familiar shaped bottle but came away empty, even the large packet of emergency Swiss chocolate had gone.

"Rupert!" Russell shouted.

"You yelled?" Rupert replied, materialising slowly from the head down.

"Someone is running around my theatre pinching things."

"And you have called me down because?"

"One of those things was a bottle of fourteen-year-old single malt which was almost half full!"

"Ah well, it is serious then."

"One of your lot is dressing up as the Phantom of the bloody Opera and is nicking comestibles?"

"Well at least he isn't ravishing nubile young sopranos and dropping chandeliers on the paying punter."

"Not yet, no ... but we have that ghost-hunter turning up in less than a week's time ..."

"I shall hold an enquiry and see what I can come up with, probably some youthful prank." And with those conciliatory words Rupert vanished, to reappear a few moments later looking decidedly ruffled.

"Er not that I think you ought to be worried or anything but none of my lot are at all responsible for any of the minor attacks of larceny, although I can't speak for Mad Harry as he's locked himself in the basement due to this television thing and you might want to have a word with the detective currently prowling around the front lobby."

"Oh, and why would I want to do that?"

"Well, Mervin says that someone has stuffed a body behind the boiler and unless it's removed fairly quickly he's going to have one of his turns ..."

"*What*!" Russell squawked, rising from his seat at the same time as Bob Callow entered his small and cluttered office.

"Is this a bad moment?" Bob asked. "Only I can come back after lunch."

* * *

Silently they stood and looked at the mangled remains of what had once been a large and fearsome thug, with a Neanderthal jawline and a morbid taste in tattoos, if the skulls and tombstones peeking from his torn clothing were any indication of the full artwork concealed upon his person.

Russell gulped and watched as Bob Callow viewed the cadaver with pursed lips and a thoughtful expression in his eyes.

"So this wasn't here early this morning?" Bob asked.

"I have no idea; it certainly wasn't here last night, because even the plumbers couldn't have missed that." Russell gulped again, swallowing down a mouthful of bile.

"And they haven't turned up this morning?"

"No, not yet, they rang earlier to say they had a burst

boiler at Grenaby and would be in later."

"Right, well the first thing to do is to ring this in and the next to secure the scene before the police turn up, which means ..." Bob added, gently pushing a protesting Russell from the room, "that nobody touches anything at all."

Chapter Seven

Tavistock arrived just as the van from the funeral directors left, and walked straight into something from one of her own highly inventive scripts. Brian Clague was trying to calm down the large lady who was in charge of props, Bob Callow was trying very hard not to take over the investigation and failing miserably, as all the younger constables were calling him 'Sir' and looking hopeful, pens poised above raised notebooks. George the carpenter had the radio at maximum to drown out the cries of anguish coming from the dressing rooms, mainly from the actors who had turned up early for the impromptu rehearsal which Tavistock's harassed husband had insisted upon. The loudest moans were from the very few, who a week before the curtain was to go up, had actually learnt their lines.

Russell had locked himself in his office and Lou Sphinx, after finally giving up on getting anyone to open the front door, had arrived backstage with an entourage in tow which was worthy of Queen Elizabeth I on one of her summer progresses, the train of which included two fairly senior middle management civil servants, one from the Department of Tourism and one from the Isle of Man Film Commission.

"More protagonists than the battle of Brunswick Road Post Office," Mannanan whispered into her left ear.

Tavistock froze and then without moving a hair hissed back, "And what may I ask are you doing here?"

"Collecting bodies. Actually we couldn't have a quiet word, could we?"

"We?"

"Upstairs."

"Where?"

"Just follow me."

Tavistock reluctantly turned from the scene of steadily mounting chaos and sidled past a young constable attempting to answer questions being spat at him by both Government officials. Nobody took any notice whatsoever of her careful negotiation of the warren of backstage corridors, no one except Bob Callow who had managed to catch Mannanan's eye as he wafted past.

Finally she was ushered into a long and dismal room, full to the brim of anxiously pacing souls; some sat in subdued silence, a few wandered around muttering and occasionally one or two dressed in fading tutus tentatively poked their heads through the wall and then, if anyone noticed, vanished just as quickly.

"Ahem ..." Mannanan coughed loudly into the mêlée. A heavy silence fell and all eyes turned as one to him.

"And now that I have your undivided attention, I'd like to ask if anyone saw anything at all this morning or yesterday evening."

"Who's she?" a skinny old woman dressed in black from

head to toe asked suspiciously.

"This is Tavistock Allan, my ... er ... assistant," Mannanan replied.

"Who?"

"Tavistock Allan, she's a writer," Mannanan shouted.

"What?"

"A writer ..." Mannanan shouted again, this time a good deal closer. The old woman glared at him.

"I heard you the first time young man, and there's no need to shout; I'm not deaf, you know."

One of the younger ghosts sighed pointedly and hid his head in his hands.

"Did you see anything?" Mannanan asked, enunciating extremely carefully so that she could lipread each word.

"Why?"

"Because someone was killed in the boiler room."

"Have you asked Mervin?"

"Not yet."

"Well, that's his room, you should ask him. I never go in there, don't go backstage at all, don't hold with them ..."

"Who?"

"Those young things, flitting about in not much at all, showing their legs and things, ain't decent. In my day ..."

"Yes, yes, I can quite understand, but did you see anything odd in the auditorium yesterday?"

"The what?"

Tavistock took a deep breath and went over to stand beside her. "What we need to know is if anything unusual happened or if any strangers turned up," Tavistock asked, moving a chair from beside the wall towards the old lady, who with a little nod and an adjustment of clothing sat down. One gnarled claw-like hand covered in black lace emerged from the folds of dark cloth and patted Tavistock's wrist.

"Anything unusual, hummm ..." They waited while she thought back to the previous night. "They struck the old set after the audience had gone ... couldn't say how many there were ... not a lot really which was a pity because it was not a bad play ... when they remembered their lines, and they had a vicar ... or it could have been a bishop. The best bit was when they all hid in the wardrobe and it fell over ... I don't think it was in the script, and the language – well, call me old-fashioned, dear, but ..."

"And then what happened after the audience had gone?" Tavistock prompted.

"I helped the lad clear up the ice-cream wrappers, I always do on a last night, been doing it seventy-odd years now and not so much as a thank you from anyone ..."

"And after the lights went out ..."

"I had a bit of a wander, stretched my legs, I can't recall anything out of the ordinary oh except that I nearly bumped into the new chap."

"New chap?"

"The one in the cloak and the mask."

"What was he doing?"

"He was taking food from behind the bar."

"So he was stealing food?"

"Well no ... not really dear, he was trying to add it all up so as to leave them the right money, only adding up doesn't appear to be his strong suit."

"Oh."

"I was a teacher, you know."

"No, no, I didn't."

"Well, a governess, but it was still teaching, still ..." The old lady's thoughts trailed away and so did she, leaving a slightly colder area around the now empty chair.

"Mask? Cloak? What new chap?" Cedric demanded, standing up and moving rapidly towards Tavistock who was still staring thoughtfully into space.

"And you are?" Mannanan asked.

"Cedric Fotherington-Bassett hyphenated. I was a director of some note and, I may add, of no little talent."

"If any at all," a sour voice interrupted.

"Oh it's you, Edwin, I should have known you'd turn up ready to hog the limelight and generally muddy the waters."

"Gentleman please, Mannanan is a very busy, er … person as is our distinguished guest so a little less bickering would go a long way."

"Ah Rupert, I wondered where you had got to," Mannanan quietly muttered to himself as he moved further into the centre of the room.

"Tavistock Allan, let me introduce you to Sir Rupert Kneale, playwright, producer and all round entrepreneur of the theatrical world, unfortunately his taste in paramours was not as good as his plays and he had a heart attack upon the discovery of his latest squeeze in the arms of another."

"And I have remained here ever since and on occasion it has been just as well. Do you remember that property company that wanted to turn this beautiful bastion of style and good taste into a hotel and shopping mall! Well, I saw to that, I can tell you."

"How?" Tavistock asked, intrigued, "I thought it was the clerk that got Tynwald all fired up?"

"And who do you think fired the clerk up?"

"Oh, I see."

"To say nothing of persuading that pontificating so-called do-gooder to not purchase the theatre for the good of the Island, good of his soul more like..."

"Oh?"

"Nothing like a bit of prestige haunting to cower the spirits, and before you ask, I didn't trespass upon your patch," Rupert muttered, giving Mannanan an uneasy glance. "I know your views on interference, not that you ever take any notice yourself of course ..."

Tavistock chuckled and Mannanan scowled.

"Anyway what I was going to say was that this phantom is not one of my members."

"Members?"

"The association of theatrical thespians or TATT for short. All members are, of course, deceased and none of them would ever raise a finger, well, a fist to a living member of the human race."

"I see ..."

"And I really don't like your tone, Mannanan old chap, I ... well ..."

"There was that incident a while back, before you were born, young Tavistock, when we had to do a certain amount of, er, hushing up and if I remember rightly a lot of cleaning ..."

"I have no authority there at all as you well know ..."

Tavistock looked from one to the other and smiled broadly, her writer's antennae were both quivering gently as the spectral ghost of a really good story shimmered in the ether.

"Well, go on then ..." she prompted.

"Besides which, Mad Harry never leaves the basement and he certainly wouldn't fart around in a cloak and a mask just in order to frighten people. I mean what would be the point, especially with a face like his?" Cedric crowed.

"Face?" Tavistock asked.

"Yes my dear, he has a face to curdle milk and terrify infants," Edwin piped up and winked at her.

"Edwin," Rupert barked warningly, "Mad Harry was unfortunately involved in a slight accident when the first theatre burnt to the ground."

"Accident?"

"He didn't leave enough time between applying the match and leaving the building," Edwin gleefully explained.

"Quite," Rupert growled. "Anyway, this isn't Harry's style and more importantly he certainly wouldn't pay for anything he took."

"Apart from the fact that he'd never leave the basement," Cedric added.

One of the dancers coughed nervously and then went red with embarrassment when everyone turned as one to stare at her.

"He, er, sometimes leaves ..." she stuttered.

"Oh?"

"On first nights he wanders about in the orchestra pit, and he, er, does things ..."

"What sort of things?" Rupert asked.

"Just things ..." she muttered and then vanished.

"Bloody ballerinas," Cedric snorted derisively.

"Anyway, it still isn't his thing," Rupert reiterated.

"Anybody got anything else to say before we go down to the basement?" Mannanan asked, making a brief note on his clipboard which had once more fleetingly appeared before silently disappearing.

"We?" Tavistock queried.

"You wanted to get a good story. Well, meeting Harry should give you enough fodder for a mini-series at the very least," Mannanan advised, marching towards the fire exit. The crowd of spectral shapes parted to allow Mannanan and Tavistock to leave and then re-formed behind them and continued whispering amongst themselves in a worried fashion until the appearance of Lou Sphinx and his entourage, whereupon they vanished, leaving behind a stale cold smell and a faint odour of elderly greasepaint and wintergreen.

Lou Sphinx stood in the doorway and sniffed long and loudly. "Ah!" he exclaimed, rubbing his hands and giving a deep chuckle of joy. "This is more like it."

"Er, like what?" A mousy-haired timorous assistant asked, looking around the dusty room with its attendant carefully hoarded rubbish in a faint and almost apologetic puzzlement.

"This! Can't you feel it?"

"Feel what?" A portly, middle-aged and bilious looking man wielding a beeping light meter complained as he explored the angles of the room. A cloud of dust descended from a portion of the ceiling above his head and he coughed loudly, before spitting a globule of dust and saliva onto the floor.

"The atmosphere in here it positively shrieks ectoplasmic activity," Lou Sphinx asserted, closing his eyes and standing with his arms outstretched in front of him. His accompanying retinue stopped and gave each other sympathetically pained looks.

"Here we bloody well go again," the soundman muttered internally, before pointedly switching off the machine which hung heavily around his neck. The last person to have interrupted the great man, by having the temerity to ping while the master was centring his inner self and contacting his spirit guide, had been metaphorically hung, drawn and quartered and was now filming red marching ants in some obscure and damply dripping jungle.

Tavistock and Mannanan who had quietly followed the entourage back into the room, stood and watched as Lou Sphinx breathed theatrically in and then out in long powerful draughts. Barty West, materialising at Mannanan's side, sidled over to the centre of everyone's attention and poked him hard in the stomach with a grimy index finger. Nothing happened.

Barty shrugged dramatically and sauntered back, whistling 'No We Have No Bananas' off-key.

Tavistock bit her lip and then as Lou Sphinx continued his breathing exercises, giggled loudly and not a little derisively. Lou Sphinx opened his eyes turned and glared at her. There was a brief pregnant pause as his retinue held its collective breath and then Brian Clague stormed into the room accompanied by Russell Gillings-Cooper, Richard Allan, one senior civil servant from the Tourist Department and a motley assortment of police constables and interested thespians he had been unable to shake off.

"And what in God's name are you lot doing?" Brian asked, looking around with no trace of humour at all. His glare finally alighted on Tavistock and he smiled evilly.

"Ah, you, I should have known!" he exclaimed, turning towards Bob Callow who had finally managed to edge into the room and gain a ringside view.

"You two always seem to be joined at the hip."

"Excuse me, but ..." Lou Sphinx began angrily.

"Did I give you permission to speak?" Brian barked,

finally losing the temper he had been desperately trying to hold on to for too long.

"Er ..." Lou Sphinx muttered his voice tailing off.

"I've a good mind to arrest the lot of you for obstruction!" Brian growled savagely. The man from the Tourist Department looked uneasily towards the door.

"Because, in case you hadn't noticed, I have a crime scene downstairs and before you ask," he snarled, watching Richard Allan with a gimlet glare, "No, I will not be allowing this place to open until I have everyone's statements and you lot have all left the building to me, my staff and the scene-of-crime wizards."

Everyone stared at him in an offended silence.

"Well then, what are you waiting for?" Brian asked. "See one of my constables, give your statements and then clear off."

He turned, and fixing Bob and Tavistock with a withering look, snapped, "All, that is, except you two, with whom I would like several well chosen words."

Tavistock and Bob stood and waited uncomfortably until everyone else apart from Brian had left, and then Bob moved tentatively towards his former colleague.

"Bad night?" Bob asked, moving a chair away from the wall and pressing Brian into it.

Brian, realising that resistance was useless, nodded and sat down on the proffered item of dilapidated furniture. He was, he knew, technically in charge of another homicide investigation and he also knew that his old boss Bob Callow had retired but the habit of passing everything onwards and upwards was still, he had to reluctantly admit to himself, almost impossible to break.

"We'd just get it off to sleep and those anti-social gits next door would start again. Mind you by that time the other one would have woken up demanding juice, toilet, whatever, which would wake junior up and then I'd have to drive around the TT course to try to get it back to sleep."

"Ah."

"Put the house on the market and everything, it's driving Caro mad having to keep it clean and tidy for the viewers, what with that and the constant feeding, crying and burping, it's driving us both nuts. Tell me …" he muttered, looking at Tavistock, "that it gets better …"

"Oh yes, it's called school, you get time off for good behaviour and hours to do everything you've put off for four years, mind you then they spend the next five to ten years catching every virus known to man and learning how to projectile vomit everywhere except the toilet bowl. It does get marginally better when they grow up and become teenagers because they live in their rooms, only come out for food or their friends and continually remind their aged parents that they have ruined their lives."

"Happy days," Bob sighed before adding, "Don't suppose you have the usual?"

"You mean flask of coffee and sundry edibles?" Tavistock replied, setting down her backpack.

"Yes," Bob boomed, "only I think that the new father here needs time out with a cup of something wet and hot, together with a slab of whatever it is in that interesting foil packet."

"Ginger and lemon cake, Kate baked it."

"Kate?" Brian muttered, taking the proffered plastic cup and slice of gooey dark brown sponge.

"Number one daughter; have to admit that when it comes to cakes I'm hopeless."

"Oh no, surely not," Brian politely remarked, his mouth

full of crumbs.

"The last cake I attempted the birds threw off the birdtable and they were rooks."

Brian grinned and then in far friendlier tones asked, "So, er, why are you both here?"

Bob shrugged and glanced at Tavistock, who replied first.

"I'm doing a piece on ghosts for the Friends of the Gaiety and …"

"I'm here sorting out security for Mr Sphinx," Bob added.

"So, just a happy coincidence?" Brian asked, taking another sip of coffee.

"Well, yes," Bob agreed. "Why?"

"No particular reason; it's just that we have a badly beaten corpse, who according to the doctor who examined the gently stiffening cadaver should be still up and running."

"Oh?" Bob and Tavistock exclaimed, looking towards Mannanan who was propping up one of the doorways with his arms folded.

"Odd really, he has all the signs of just dropping down dead and the doc reckons – strictly off the record and before he opens him up properly – that the only possible explanation could be that someone frightened him to death."

"Ah …"

"… Frightened him to death and then smashed him to a pulp, oddly enough particularly around the face and head."

"Oh."

"Still the double act I see," Brian observed ruefully. "I suppose it would be pointless for me to ask for the real reason you both turn up almost as soon as the corpse is discovered?"

"Completely and utterly nothing to do with either of us," Bob asserted.

"Oh."

"I don't suppose you know who the recently departed was?" Bob tentatively asked.

"Well now, there we may have a bit of a breakthrough, as one of the lads recognised some of the more lurid tattoos and reckons that he could be a local thug by the name of one Daryl Smith, who funnily enough does freelance jobs of dubious legality for one Bartholomew West, who surprise, surprise, appears to have been one of the previous owners of a property where another body has very recently been unearthed or strictly speaking, un-concreted." Brian grinned at his own joke and Mannanan, who had found himself the centre of both Tavistock and Bob's attention, shrugged and then in turn glared at the unfortunate wraith of Barty West who was beginning to look pale and uncomfortable.

"Nuffin to do wiv me guv, Scout's honour and all that," Barty whined.

"Hummph," Mannanan growled.

"And he turns up behind a boiler in the theatre?" Bob asked.

"Yes."

"Odd," Bob muttered thoughtfully.

"Why?"

"Nothing really."

"No?"

"Well, nothing that you'd believe."

"Considering the time I spent by my wife's bedside in hospital after the mad druid had attacked and nearly killed her, plus that time we blew up half a cliff-face and then rescued a mad writer with cannibalistic tendencies and a penchant for dubious sexual practices, I'd say try me," Brian advised, taking a final bite of cake.

"I ... er ... have reason to believe that the ... er ... body you ... er ... found in the cellar may actually be that of the original Bartholomew West."

"And your grounds are ..."

"Nothing concrete as yet."

"Very funny. Anything else?"

"It's just an idea and only a tentative one at that, only this advocate that's gone missing – any chance that he might have had something to do with the original and real Barty West?"

"Ah, I think I see a glimmer of daylight."

"I thought you might."

Brian handed back the newly drained cup with a grin, and looking momentarily happier and younger, rose from his wooden seat and marched purposely towards the door. "And no funny business!" he barked at them both before he departed into the gloom of the outer corridor.

"That lad doesn't trust me any more," Bob sniffed, finishing off his own coffee.

"I wonder why?" Tavistock observed before adding, "Oh no you don't, mister," as Barty West began to evaporate.

"You want us to help you prove you were murdered?"

"Er, yes," Barty whimpered, looking uneasily towards Mannanan who was carefully cleaning his nails with a small sliver of wood.

"Good, because we have a few questions we would like answered and if we don't like the answers our mutual friend reckons he can do you a nice aphid."

Barty gulped and then sank down onto the vacated chair.

"All right then," he grumbled, "what do you want to know?"

★ ★ ★

Richard Allan stood on the pavement outside the back of the theatre and watched the shadows flitting past the gnarled and bobbled glass, which separated the dressing rooms from the real world, with a mixture of barely repressed fury and outright despair. He'd actually taken a week off work to direct and produce this wretched play and now, as well as the usual problems of a cast who could barely remember their lines and a stage crew that took the simple word incompetent to hitherto unknown heights, he had a dead body to contend with. He'd almost exploded when Russell had scurried up to tell him the bad news, all that work and for what? That was why he'd tried to track down the policeman in charge; how on earth was he supposed to know that Bob had retired and that assistant of his had been put in charge? He could still remember Brian Clague as a lowly police constable covered in acne and sporting a pristine uniform pressed each morning by his devoted mother. And then suddenly and without warning there he was, all grown up, spitting venom and sporting what looked like designer stubble and the mien of an experienced Russian tyrant.

There was no way that they would be ready in time for the first night, no way.

Marianna sailed to a stop beside him and offered him a cigarette. Richard sadly shook his head. It was nearly twenty years since he had given up the evil weed but just at this particular moment he could really have done with its comforting fug.

"I saw your wife upstairs," Marianna remarked.

"Humph."

"Is she writing another one of her books?"

"Something for the Friends of the Gaiety, or so she said," Richard frowned as he remembered that Bob Callow had also been there.

"It's weird, isn't it?" Marianna remarked, casually blowing a smoke ring up towards the cloudless blue sky above their heads.

"What?"

"That your wife always seems to turn up when the cadaver does."

"I hadn't really noticed," Richard replied before hastily changing the subject.

"Have you any idea where the rest of the cast went?"

"I think they all cleared off to the villa for a coffee."

"Good, I think I'll join them and then we can all sit outside in this glorious sunshine and ..."

"Have another bloody rehearsal," Marianna interjected with a growl.

Chapter Eight

Tony threw back the opera cloak and with a dramatic chuckle pounced upon the hamper.

"Fortnum and Mason," he muttered to himself as he feverishly undid the buckles and loosened the strap. "Now I wonder what delightful goodies you have in store for hungry old me."

He threw the lid back and then stared in disbelief at the polystyrene globules.

"Oh, bugger it!" he exclaimed, sitting abruptly on the floor in a heap.

"You'd think that if it said Fortnum's on the outside it could at least contain something edible on the inside, even if it was in a tin … I even have an opener," he snarled, waving the silver implement he'd found in one of the upper dressing rooms.

"Never mind, lad," Mad Harry whispered soothingly.

"Never mind! Never mind! I'm so hungry I could eat a rat, and can I find one of them …"

Tony banged the basket in front of him so hard it tipped

and something small and round fell out. Tony stared at it in fascinated horror and licked his suddenly dry lips with the tip of his tongue.

"What play did you say they were mangling this time?" he asked.

"'Blithe Spirit'. Why?"

"Well, correct me if I'm wrong, but does it anywhere require the actual shooting of any member of the cast?"

"You'd have to ask the director about that, lad." Mad Harry answered as he sauntered around the dimly lit room. "But I'd say offhand that no one gets shot. Why?"

"Because I think that what just fell out was the silencer for a rifle."

"What!"

"In which case the rest of it must be in here." Mad Harry hurried over to where Tony was feverishly searching inside the hamper; pieces of polystyrene flew around the room like large glossy strangely shaped snowflakes until the complete gun was revealed.

"I found the bullets!" Tony exclaimed, as he sat panting beside his unearthed loot.

"Are they live ones?"

"Oh yes."

"How the hell do you know?"

"My father did a lot of shooting; he was in the army for years then the territorials, weekends away in Scotland, weeks in Kenya. I know what a rifle looks like all right and this one, I'd say, is state of the art and extremely lethal."

"What's that?" Harry asked, pointing to a contraption of plastic, perspex and fine metal.

"That, I think, is a night sight, something you can use in the dark to help you see your victim of choice."

"So you could hide in the gloom and shoot someone?"

"Oh yes, with this little lovely you could hide in the dark and hit any part you damm well wanted, including the head, the heart or the testicles."

"Why would you hide it in a theatre prop room?"

"Well if you were going to kill someone in the theatre this place would be really handy. I'd hazard a guess that somebody on this side of the stage wants to knock off someone watching from the other."

"Some unsuspecting member of the audience ..."

"Yes, probably one of the invited dignitaries, although having seen some performances I could be wrong and it might be one of the cast." Tony carefully put the night sight down and picked up the long metallic tube upon which it had to be screwed.

Mad Harry watched him competently rebuild what was fast becoming a very sleek and businesslike weapon with a worried frown. Finally it was finished and Tony placed it carefully on the dusty floor.

"So what do we do now?" Tony asked, removing his mask and scratching his chin where the bristles were growing in profusion.

"Put it all back and have a bit of a think," Mad Harry answered, collecting stray bits of packaging in semi-transparent hands.

"You don't think that somehow those men have found out where I am?" Tony queried as he set about disassembling the gun.

"No lad, I don't; as far as I know they don't have a clue as to your whereabouts, but I'll tell you this for nothing, somebody in this place is running around with a great big target emblazoned all over their chest and they don't even know it."

"I heard some of the cast talking about that television presenter today and most of them would quite happily have used something like this," Tony rumbled, replacing the last of the rifle parts and covering them with polystyrene shavings.

"Which is why they probably don't know about this ... As it's my opinion the person that had this delivered will be staying very quiet, very quiet indeed."

"Are you sure?"

"Oh yes, absolutely," Mad Harry asserted, helping to close the lid while Tony re-fixed the binding and buckles.

"Harry?"

"What?"

"I'm still hungry."

"I'll find you something else, bound to be something lying around in the dressing rooms."

Tony and Harry carefully sidled from the room and tiptoed around the perimeter of the theatre, their minds half-turned towards their unlikely find.

* * *

"That bloody awful, bloody man!" Russell moaned as he sat slumped at his desk with his head in his hands.

"Which bloody awful man? I mean to say, there are so many," Rupert asked, leaning over the glass of whisky that Russell had poured himself, which was slowly evaporating across the paper-strewn surface of his cluttered desk.

"Ahh ..." Rupert declared appreciatively, as the waft of a fine single malt drifted up and through him.

"That awful Sphinx character." Russell took a long and large gulp of Balvenie and, closing his eyes, shuddered at various recent memories.

"Well, I admit that he is pretty appalling."

"Appalling! My dear Rupert, calling that … that man, appalling doesn't even come close to describing him. That insufferable oaf has actually taken it upon himself to move almost the entire current cast out of their dressing rooms and had all their stuff transported to the other rooms on the upper floor. Richard understandably threw an almighty wobble at having his flock upset – after all it's one thing shouting at your own cast of idiot thespians but it's quite another having some complete stranger do it – and stormed into one of my management meetings threatening to cancel the show and we could basically sing for our money. I wouldn't have minded so much but he'd managed to include that anarchist from the Arts Council and She Who Must Be Obeyed from the Drama Federation. And that wasn't the worst bit, oh no, our Richard when he's not wielding the baton of direction here, is castigating non-payers of taxes and misappropriaters of forms for the Financial Supervision Commission so the majority of illiterate morons comprising the committee were actually terrified of the wretched man."

"Ah."

"That's what's so bloody wrong about letting the amateurs in, most of them have better jobs than me." Russell gave another heartfelt sigh and took another swallow of amber nectar.

"Can't you do something?"

"What?"

"I don't know. Cancel the TV thing? Say you can't possibly allow Mr Sphinx in as he's had death threats and you already have one deceased body on your plate already. I don't suppose you want to start a collection?"

"No."

"Ahh."

"Anyway, I already put in my complaint to the higher echelons of tourism and it was like hitting a wall with a very small lime jelly."

"Didn't want to know?"

"Deaf in every orifice and that's including both ears."

"So no change there then."

"They said that it was good for business, that I was being overcautious and that I could move 'Blithe Spirit' to next week."

"Oh."

"Next week is when we have that professional theatre company over from Liverpool, everything is already booked including their accommodation, we even have a healthy sale in advance tickets, so I can't possibly cancel it."

"Did you have a word with Richard?"

"Oh yes and all he said was 'Well two can play at that game; if it's war that shower wants then it's war they are going to get, let me know when the police say we can come back in.' And then he cleared off, looking like he'd personally like to wring someone's neck with his bare hands, and to put the icing on the thing, that wretched phantom stole Mr Sphinx's lunch, personally made for him by his own staff. The assistant is apparently in hysterics and Mr Sphinx is talking about having a press conference and then catching the phantom himself."

"Well, good luck to him on that particular count; I've been trying to hunt the wretched creature down all morning and have achieved absolutely nothing and I'm dead."

"Exactly."

"So what will you do?"

"In the short term I'm going to get ever so slightly drunk and then ... I'm going to get really plastered."

* * *

Mannanan moved down the stairs to the basement and at the bottom stopped, there was a distinct iciness in the quality of the stagnant air and it was coming from the direction of the area directly under the stage.

Tavistock and Bob joined him and stood silently letting their eyes adjust to the gloom.

Brian, who had followed them from the boiler room, cleared his throat loudly.

"So this is where all the old Victorian stage thingies live?"

"Yes," Tavistock whispered, listening intently to the spreading silence.

"There's someone in there," Mannanan muttered.

"You'd better go and take a look then," Bob hissed, the hairs on the back of his neck rippling uncomfortably.

Mannanan vanished and then they heard shouting followed by a crash.

"What the hell was that?" Brian yelled, thrusting his shoulder against the wooden door, which was firmly locked from the inside.

"I have no idea, but whatever it is it's met its match by the sound of things," Tavistock replied as she leant against the dank whitewashed wall and listened intently.

Mad Harry stood amongst the ropes and pulleys of mechanisms designed to lift and lower entire choruses and scowled horribly; he could feel the power in the enclosed wood filled space and for once it wasn't emanating from him.

"Who are you?" he asked.

"Nobody you really want to upset. Now go and open that door before I really lose my temper," Mannanan replied, toying with the idea of a small fireball.

Mad Harry turned towards one of the renovated wooden lifts. The lad was very obviously not at all well and he had no idea why.

"If I do, and it's a big if, you go easy on the lad. He paid for everything he took and it's not as if anyone was harmed."

"And the thug in the boiler room?"

"That may have been me …"

"Oh."

"He was after the lad and all I did was have a quiet word with him."

"Which was?"

"*Boo*!"

"Oh."

"How was I to know he had a weak heart?"

"Right."

"I blame the modern diet, not enough fibre and red meat: meat and at least two veg, mug or two of stout and you could go on for years, now it's all peel off the wrapper and ping – it's ready."

"The door?"

"Right, and the lad …"

"I'll do what I can."

Tavistock, Bob and Brian almost fell into the room as it was thrown open and stared into the gloom. A light went on, illuminating a wealth of wooden struts and supports harbouring what looked like the ordinary sadist's wet dream of pulleys, ropes and wheels. From a particularly lethal crib of wood and rope a groan emanated.

"Who's there?" Tavistock asked, moving carefully towards the sound.

Bob sidled around a hefty beam which appeared to disappear directly up and into the stage floor above their heads and then stopped abruptly as he saw the figure curled into the foetal position within the sturdy confines of one of the underground traps.

"Isn't this the one called the Corsican Trap?" he asked, rubbing a hand down the dry wood.

"Originally built for the play 'The Corsican Brothers'," Mad Harry advised in a proprietorial fashion.

"Ah, I've seen it work, that time they disinterred the scripts for the centenary celebrations."

"And what did you think of it?" Mad Harry asked.

"Frankly the play was bloody awful but the trap was really good, apart from the fact that they were still attempting to move a sofa off set when it started up, rather spoilt the effect I thought."

"Ah yes, well I can see that it might have been a little offputting," Harry agreed, gazing upwards.

"Look, I don't know whether you've noticed but there's a bloke in there dressed up in an opera cloak and a mask and he really doesn't look at all well," Brian hissed, pushing past them to where Tavistock was kneeling at the side of the writhing body.

"How long has he been like this?" she demanded, carefully removing the white plastic mask from his head.

"Ever since lunch," Mad Harry replied, a degree of worry evident in his voice.

"What did he eat?" Tavistock asked, shining a torch in the man's eyes which were heavily dilated.

"A beef sandwich."

"Just beef?"

"No, there was some sort of sauce, horseradish I think although ... he did say it tasted a bit bitter."

"Horseradish!" Tavistock scoffed and then felt the man's wrist for a pulse. She frowned and sitting back on her heels demanded, "and just where did it come from?"

"What, the horseradish?"

"No you moron, the bloody sandwich!" she shouted. Mad Harry winced and then after a brief pause muttered, "I think it was from one of the dressing rooms."

"Not the one belonging to Lou Sphinx?" Bob asked.

"Dunno, the lad just appeared with a plate in his hand. He was really pleased because they were his favourites, apparently his wife don't make them very often as he's the only one that likes horseradish."

"Did he leave any?" Bob asked.

"No, pigged the lot," Mad Harry replied, appearing almost pleased about his protégé's appetite.

"Well, I can tell you one thing, what he ate wasn't all horseradish; my guess is that the sauce was laced with finely grated Belladonna root," Tavistock advised.

"What!" Bob, Brian and Harry replied in almost perfect harmony.

"We have to make him sick," Mannanan muttered, bending over the cloaked form which had now started to twitch.

"Hang on a bit, before we do that I need to know a few things," Tavistock replied. "What symptoms did he get after eating the sandwich?"

"Well, he said his throat felt a bit sore and his mouth was dry, so I gave him a drink."

"And then what?"

"His eyes went all funny and his face looked a bit flushed

– what I could see of it – and then he started groaning and … well … rambling," Mad Harry answered. "He is going to be all right, isn't he?"

"That all depends on whether we can make him sick and get him into hospital as soon as possible."

"And what if I don't want him to go?"

"If you don't help us he could, depending on the dosage, die."

"Die?" Mad Harry took a step back.

"If it is belladonna, and the root was added to the horse-radish he'll develop a high fever, possibly convulsions, will fall into a coma and then die … that is if his heart doesn't stop first," Tavistock uttered darkly.

"How the hell do you know? It could just be a bit of rancid beef," Harry barked at her.

"I know because I've just spent nearly a month researching the death of Alexander the Great, who was supposedly poisoned by one of the alkaloids; I personally have pinned my colours to strychnine but other writers have also worked on a tincture of belladonna or a concoction of aconite."

"Oh."

"And your pal here has all the initial symptoms of belladonna poisoning and at a rough guess I'd say whoever spiked the edibles was working on at least ten guinea pigs," Tavistock replied as she peered at her mobile phone. The hand clasping hers twitched and then shuddered horribly.

"Argh, no signal. Someone go and find something to make him throw up; the old method used to be a large glass of saltwater or mustard in water, especially as he hasn't been sick yet himself, oh and if possible a very strong black coffee, caffeine apparently was considered an antidote … and get an ambulance."

"Why would anyone want to poison him?" Harry asked.

"I don't think they set out to get your friend but I'd lay odds on the fact that he pinched his lunch from Lou Sphinx's dressing room," Bob grunted as he quickly made his way back towards the basement door.

"Hang on …" Brian panted as he followed him at almost a run. "Why would someone do that?"

"Because they've tried it before," Bob replied, taking the stairs up towards the backstage area three at a time.

"Why the hell did no one tell me?" Brian shouted as they made it to the back door and a welcome signal from Manx Pronto.

"Because … Yes I need an ambulance … it's an emergency, a possible poisoning … the Gaiety Theatre… yes DI ….er, Bob Callow … thanks." Bob disconnected and looked up at his quietly seething ex-partner. "Er, the thing is they didn't want you to know about it because of the press and you might have had certain well-founded concerns about his safety, apart from which no one was at all sure that he hadn't attempted to kill himself purely in the interests of self-publicity."

"Publicity – what sort of nut would do that?" Brian asked, slightly mollified.

"The sort of nut that is in the habit of talking to dead people for money, the sort who has for various reasons of publicity – and please don't enlighten me as to what sort of reader they would appeal to – has had himself sealed up in a supposedly haunted crypt for a week completely naked and with only a torch, seven litres of water and a camera for company."

"Naked?"

"And at his age."

"We are talking about Lou Sphinx here, aren't we?"

"Yes."

"The mind boggles; you'd think he'd have worn underpants."

"Actually, considering it was in Edinburgh, at least two sets of thermals and a forty-tog duvet."

"What did he want the camera for?"

"So he could take pictures of anything interesting that came up."

"And did it?" Brian asked, grinning broadly.

"You have a mind like a sew ..." Bob stopped as he could clearly hear the earpiercing klaxon of an approaching ambulance as it negotiated the corner of Finch Road with a squeal of brakes and snarl of gears. It roared towards them and then stopped, disgorging two luridly clad paramedics clutching a fold-up stretcher and a plastic medical bag.

"In there?" one of them asked, recognising Brian.

"Basement. I'll show you," Brian added, and then disappeared into the gloom of the backstage area.

"Excuse me but ..." a timid voice asked, as Brian and the medics departed clinking gently into the darkness.

Bob turned and fixed the speaker with a thoughtful stare. He was used to summing up people quickly and efficiently often using only five categories; good witness, bad witness, guilty as sin, victim and completely useless. The lady in front of him however was giving him pause for thought as she was almost completely grey in quality. Neutral voice, expression and one of those plain, worried, middle-aged faces which would disturb nobody's dreams and probably never had.

Bob watched her carefully and then after extracting a box of Tic-tacs from his pocket took one and chewed methodically. After about a minute he asked, "What?"

"I'm sorry?" the woman beside him asked, startled. She clutched at her hand-knitted cardigan and viewed him with nervous pale eyes.

"Do you want?" Bob completed his original question and regarded her thoughtfully.

"I, er, heard that someone had been taken ill."

"Oh."

"The stage manager told me."

"And you are?"

"Mr Sphinx's assistant. Well, at least I'm one of them," she added hurriedly.

"Right," Bob remarked. A tic had started working at the side of one of his companion's eyebrows.

"I just wondered if ..."

"What?"

"If it was because of something they had eaten?"

"Why ask me?"

"Well I ... aren't you that private detective, the one hired to look after Mr Sphinx?"

"And what if I am?"

"I just thought you'd like to know that his sandwiches have disappeared from his dressing room. Mr Sphinx has only just found out and he told them, I mean me, to find out what had happened and if ... well, if they were eaten then I'll have found out won't I?"

"I suppose so, but why don't I tell him myself?"

"Well I ..." She bit her lip nervously and looked timorously towards one of the opaque windows to their left, from which the muted sounds of shouting could be heard although the actual words were indistinguishable.

"Don't you worry about it, I'll see that Mr Sphinx is fully

informed about the situation. In fact I positively insist that I'm the first person to regale him with the details," he grinned down at her quaking form and then, after patting her gently on the shoulder, negotiated his way around the men trying to open the main door to allow the stretcher through.

He stood outside Mr Sphinx's door and listened with pleasure to the altercation going on inside, the other eavesdroppers having previously scurried away as soon as they realised who Bob Callow actually was.

Bob knocked and then without waiting for a reply entered.

"This,' he thought, regarding the steely-eyed combatants, "is going to be fun."

* * *

Russell Gillings-Cooper stood surrounded by the wooden supports to the various trapdoors above his head and regarded Tavistock Allan, Detective Inspector Brian Clague and Mad Harry with a jaundiced eye.

"So that was the phantom, was it?" he asked, bending to retrieve the scarlet-lined opera cloak and white plastic mask.

"We believe so, yes," Brian replied, leaning against one of the uprights.

"I wonder why he chose to live down here?" Tavistock asked of no one in particular.

Russell gave a mild start as Mad Harry winked at him.

Tavistock, observing the exchanged glance, regarded him thoughtfully before asking "So you can see Harry too, can you?"

"I ... er ... well that is ... it's sort of part of the job, unofficially that is, I mean you have to sort of live with them if you see what I mean …" His voice tailed off as Brian who was now regarding him in the manner of a scientist with a new bug, moved towards him.

"You see ghosts?" he asked, deliberately avoiding Tavistock's eye.

"You needn't sound like that," Russell squeaked.

"Like what?"

"Like you think I'm mad." Brian said nothing but his eyes agreed with Russell's comment.

"I'm not even slightly insane, just a little more psychically attuned to the spirit world than you obviously are. And anyway …" he continued, "she can see them too and you don't appear to regard her as in need of therapy and a long lie-down."

"Did I say that you were potty?"

"Well no, but you looked like you were thinking it."

"If you had seen what I've seen over the last five years you'd realise that you don't even qualify for the title 'mildly nutty'."

"Oh."

"He helped catch the mad druid and he apprehended the Glashton," Tavistock helpfully advised.

"Not all on my own," Brian interjected.

"Well no, I do admit that you did have help in blowing up that cliff-face and …" Tavistock agreed, warming to her subject.

"Exactly."

"Er, right," Russell remarked, regarding them both with a certain degree of puzzlement.

"You have absolutely no idea what we are talking about, do you?" Tavistock asked.

"Well no, not really."

"Don't you read the news?"

"Only *The Times* Arts pages and an occasional copy of *Private Eye* and *The Spectator* oh and *Vanity* of course."

"Of course."

"I mean, I do occasionally peruse that repulsively addictive *Hello* magazine but only for the more interesting titbits of gossip."

"As do we all," Tavistock murmured.

"I think we're beginning to stray from the main point," Brian snapped. "Do you have any idea who the man masquerading as the phantom was?"

"No," Russell replied. "I have never …" he stopped as a thought hit him, "although he did look vaguely familiar, strangely enough I could almost visualize him with a tennis racket and a top hat, although not at the same time."

"And that makes so much sense," Brian muttered complainingly.

"What I meant was that I think he may have been one of the many amateur thespians who hire the theatre."

"Oh." Brian rubbed his nose thoughtfully. "Well, that would certainly tie in with the Phantom's knowledge of the theatre.

"Er …" Tavistock murmured as Mannanan whispered in her ear and then stood back to regard the effect that his words had had. "He could very well be that advocate you'd like to have words with; the one you need to ask about the body found on Douglas beach and, er, he was Bartholomew West's legal adviser. The real West, not the one currently signing the cheques or employing the thug you found behind the boiler. Oh, and whoever mangled him did it after the victim died."

"After the victim died?" Brian reiterated.

"Definitely afterwards," Tavistock replied, as Mad Harry firmly nodded his head in affirmation.

"And you know this because a load of dead people I can't see are giving you their expert witness statements?" Brian growled.

"Er, yes."

"And I will be able to write this up how?" Brian asked in despairing tones.

"Ask Bob, he must have had a lot of practice," Tavistock remarked as they wandered back towards the basement stairs. They were almost at the door when Mad Harry caught up with them and blocked the doorway. Brian, suddenly finding himself standing on the inside of an invisible freezer, stopped and looked at Tavistock for support. Tavistock, deep in conversation with someone he could still not see, had paled as she appeared to be listening avidly to the starkly illuminated doorway. Finally she turned and gave him a shortened version of Mad Harry's monologue. "Er, you may not be overjoyed to hear this, but Mad Harry and his young apprentice have discovered a sniper's rifle complete with night sight, silencer and ammunition in a hamper in the props room."

"Oh," Brian replied, "a real one, not a prop?" he added hopefully.

"No, it is most definitely of the real and working variety."

"Then Harry had better show us where it is."

Tavistock followed Harry through the theatre's gloomy hinterland until she and her shadow, Brian, stood in front of the offending wicker trunk. Silently they unpacked it after carefully each putting on the nylon gloves that Brian always kept in his capacious pockets.

"Well, it's definitely a weapon of some sort," Brian announced as the pieces lay spread on the floor in front of him. Tavistock, who was crouched down beside him, nodded.

"You stay here and guard it with your life while I find someone to contact Firearms and have it safely taken away," Brian ordered.

Tavistock nodded again in agreement and sat back on her haunches.

"Do you think that the lad will be ... well ... better soon?" Mad Harry asked from his position on a pile of sagging boxes in the corner.

"I think so, yes. I mean, I think we got to him in time, I just hope that the poor sod this is meant for has the same luck," Tavistock replied thoughtfully.

Some time later Brian returned and together he and Tavistock went in search of Bob Callow. They emerged from the nether regions at almost the same time as Bob was forcibly ejected from Lou Sphinx's dressing-room.

Bob and Brian silently regarded each other, Bob because Brian was wearing a large cobweb on his head and Brian because Bob's nose was bearing a faint trickle of blood.

"Er, Bob?" Brian began, handing him a paper tissue.

"I know, I know, but you should see the other fellah."

Chapter Nine

Despite the protestations of Mr Lou Sphinx, his entourage and the man from the Ministry, Brian Clague took matters into his own hands and frogmarched Mr Sphinx from the theatre. Completely unrepentant and wearing the outward mien of an experienced Spanish Inquisitor he stormed past the waiting paparazzi, which consisted of a well known local hack and his travelling photographer, two tourists and an opportunist van driver with a mobile phone, and after a brief drive escorted a chastened and largely silent celebrity into the nearest available interview room.

"I want my lawyer!" Lou Sphinx shouted as the door closed behind him with a metallic clang.

"Sit down and shut up," Brian shouted back.

Lou Sphinx glared at him in angry surprise and sat abruptly upon the nearest available item of utilitarian fur niture.

"Go on then, read me my rights," Lou demanded, folding his arms across his chest and pushing his chair back from the table.

"No," Brian flatly replied, beckoning to the police constable who was standing next to the door.

"I'd like a large white Americano, two sugars and some sort of sandwich without tomatoes or mayonnaise or any sort of gunk." Brian searched around in his pocket and extracted a wealth of coins which he began to sort out on the table. "And a slice of ginger cake or the carrot thing."

"And I'll have a large Cappuccino, two sugars and a slice of chocolate cake if they have it," Lou Sphinx added.

"Er, that'll be about four pounds," The gangly youth muttered.

"What?"

"He goes to the coffee shop across the road, but if you'd prefer you can have something made on the premises. After all, I believe that the stomach pump is still in storage," Brian muttered, handing over a collection of coins.

"Ah, a pessimist."

"No, a realist," Brian replied, sitting back and glaring at him in a hostile fashion.

"So when are you going to read me my rights and get me a lawyer?" Lou asked.

"When you need one," Brian snapped.

There was a gentle tap on the door, followed by the tentative entrance of a young woman clutching a wad of papers which she silently handed to Brian who sighed and then began to read each one very, very slowly. Lou Sphinx watched her about-turn and softly close the door behind her; he gave a low wolf whistle and drummed his fingers on the table.

"She's married and a civilian so don't give me any rubbish about liking women in uniform," Brian advised, turning over a page. "You may also be interested to know that her husband is a well known local roofer and he'd snap you like a twig."

"Oh."

"I suppose we could sell tickets, probably be able to pay for a complete wing of the new hospice on the proceeds of seeing someone beat you to a pulp," Brian remarked thoughtfully as his gaze scanned a long list of names, some of which had notes of further names scribbled in the margin.

"You don't like me much, do you?" Lou asked.

"I don't actually like you at all," Brian replied, sitting back and studying him.

"So why am I here?" asked Lou.

"You are, as I informed the press, helping us with our enquiries," Brian rumbled, whilst searching for a pen in one of his many pockets.

"I don't see why I had to leave my dressing room to do it," Lou grumbled.

"Because Forensics need to be able to powder in peace," Brian retorted, striking one of the names from the list with a flourish. "Apart from which, I had every reason to believe that witnesses may have been more willing to talk without you around."

"Oh."

"I have never had two choruses of 'For He's a Jolly Good Fellah' sung in my honour when taking someone into custody before."

"Ah, custody, huh? I am a suspect."

"I should have said 'protective custody'."

"But …"

"Look Mr Sphinx, let's get one thing absolutely and crystal clear shall we? I don't like you but on the other hand I would like the flak heaped upon me by my elders and not necessarily betters in the event of your early demise even less."

"My what!"

"A round of sandwiches made to your order and left in your dressing room was, we suspect, laced with something other than horseradish and the unlucky little sod who ate them is at this present moment undergoing intensive medical intervention. I personally couldn't care less if you shuffled off this mortal coil but the powers-that-be would prefer it if you did it off Island."

"Shit."

"Exactly. It may also interest you to know that we found a fully working and absolutely lethal fire arm hidden inside the Gaiety Theatre, a firearm designed to kill in the dark and with very little noise, something a professional would give quite a lot of hard-earned and bloody cash for."

Lou Sphinx paled and then stammered, "A gun?"

"With more than two bullets so that presumably he or indeed she could have another go if they failed to eliminate you the first time."

"And you found this ... gun where?"

"In a hamper in the props room, someone had sent it in with a consignment of costumes and theatrical accoutrements from a central warehouse in Liverpool."

"Liverpool." Lou sagged against his chairs and closed both eyes with a distinct shudder.

"But who would want to do that?"

"Ah, I'm so glad you said that; I have a list which I'd like to go through with you."

"A list?"

"Two sides of A4 and with narrow margins."

"As many as that?"

"Oh yes, mind you, apparently they haven't included the entire population of a small village in Gwent but doubtless they have their reasons, economy probably."

Lou Sphinx regarded his tormentor with a suddenly deflated look and shrank into his seat. It was at that point that the refreshment arrived with a receipt and two mounds of change, the lesser handed to Brian with a folded note. Brian read it and then, frowning, looked up. "Are they sure?" he asked.

"Absolutely positive."

"Right, you'd better bring your lunch back in and sit down with us, this may take some time. By the way how is the poor little sod?"

"Recovering slowly. Apparently if he'd been left much longer …"

"Right."

Brian unwrapped the sandwich in front of him and grinned with pleasure. "Good roast beef and no gunk."

"What poor sod?" Lou asked, his upper lip ringed with froth.

"The one that pinched your lunch," Brian replied. "Apparently he'd ingested enough belladonna root to kill him but fortunately the administered caffeine and subsequent pumping out of the stomach stopped him actually joining our steadily increasing murder statistics."

"Which are?"

"Thankfully not into double figures as yet."

"Oh."

"So we'll start at the beginning of this hate list and try and find out who actually wants you dead."

"I suppose so." Lou Sphinx shrugged and took a bite

out of his chocolate slice. "God, but that's good," he announced, looking slightly happier.

"Hummm, who is Winona Gracewold?" Brian asked.

"My ex-wife."

"And Sharon Gould?"

"Another ex-wife."

Brian exchanged a look of incredulous amusement with the young constable and then asked, "And Gloria Medcalf?"

"Wife number four."

"And what happened to wife number three?"

"She died."

"Oh."

"Which was something I was and still am very upset about."

"Why?"

"I liked her."

"Right." Brian made a short note against wives one, two and four and struck a line through number three. "And just exactly how many ex-wives do you currently have?"

"At the moment only the four."

"Not thinking of increasing the ranks then?"

"Not after Gloria, no ..."

"And this change of a lifetime is because ..."

"She went for me with a pitchfork."

"Make a note to interview Ms Medcalf first."

"And all I said was ..."

"What?"

"Nothing, it doesn't matter ..." he sulkily replied.

"And make another note to ask her what started the argument," Brian added.

"I have next on my list of suspects a Captain Charles Morris?"

"Ah ..."

"That doesn't help."

"Do you really need to know?"

"Either you tell us or somebody else will."

"I suppose so. Morris was Sharon's husband."

"And I presume that he was still her husband when ..."

"He caught us in my trailer."

"Oh."

"There was a bit of a scene and then he stormed off and then married my first wife."

"Keeping it in the family."

"So to speak, they still both loathe me."

"I wonder why?"

"There is no need to use that tone with me, Detective," Lou sniffed.

"Why not? You use it all the time," Brian remarked. "Any other ex-husbands, lovers and other persons on this list?"

"Brian Pilkington, Dave Lawson and Chris Le Grande and possibly Kiki West."

"Kiki?"

"He was married to my assistant Cheryl until he had a short holiday in Holland; things went apart after he came back."

"I'm not sure I really want to know."

"To be honest neither did Cheryl, which I guess was part of the problem; anyway last I heard he'd bought a sheep station in Australia."

"Right. Adam, did you get all that? Good, now write down cuckold against each one, it will save time later."

"Now look here ..."

"If you want to go, there's the door, you can be my guest, only it just might be safer in here."

"It was just one sandwich."

"So you really did cut your own brakeline and spike your own drink with glass splinters?"

"No, of course not!"

"Rumour has it that both of the aforementioned attempts upon your life were done by you for the resultant publicity."

"I'll sue you for every penny that …" Lou spluttered until Brian glanced at him with barely concealed exasperation and crossed out another name.

"And who have you just crossed off that list?" Lou demanded.

"You."

"Oh."

"And as you seem so eager to resort to the legal process, how many of these are the unhappy participants in various litigious affairs?"

"I … Oh very well, although they may not be on that list …"

"Let's find out, shall we?"

"Peter and Susan Galbraith, they called me a cunning shyster with the morals of a particularly lecherous … I forget the rest, but it nearly bankrupted them when I took them to court and I think that she had some sort of breakdown or he did."

"Anybody else?"

"My lawyer would have the full list of … er … actions."

"And he is …?"

"Er … it's actually a she, and very efficient she is too, I really rather fancied her as wife number five but she declined on the grounds of professional etiquette."

"Should I add her to the list then?" Brian asked, pen poised.

"Probably."

"Robert Smith is underlined twice – why?"

"He said that I was instrumental in the suicide of his daughter."

"And were you?"

"How could I have been, I never ever met her."

"Then why?"

"He said that she had taken one of my programmes to heart and just wanted to be with her boyfriend, who died in a car crash, speeding or something. It was last September, my assistant will be able to get you a copy. I watched it over and over again but I still have no idea what he was going on about, he's just another nutter."

"How many nutters are there?"

"I get about twenty letters a week from the fringe of insanity and a further five or so from the truly deranged."

"Why do you carry on?"

"It's a job, it's what I do."

"Have you any idea about the identity of your would-be assassin."

"No."

Brian sighed, and then on reading down the page, stopped at a name and fixed Lou Sphinx with a puzzled frown.

"Bartholomew West?"

"Oh, him."

"Yes him."

"He's Kiki West's brother."

"I see, and he blames you for the breakdown of his brother's marriage?"

"Hardly, considering he was screwing Cheryl years before I met her."

"So why is he here?"

"He didn't want me to make a programme about Denton Wood Apartments."

Brian stared blankly at him. "Why?"

"Because they fell down. He built them and they fell down, killed quite a few people, squatters and the like. When I asked him for his views he just shrugged and said they shouldn't have been there, but they were paying him rent, or rather his collectors. I found a witness, a relative of one of the deceased, she'd grown up since the disaster, got a job – as a researcher funnily enough – actually it was her idea to go down there talking to the dead."

"And did you?"

"In the end, no; somebody, somewhere pulled a few strings and it never happened. She blamed me so perhaps she ought to go on the list. Why do you want to know?"

"Because the body we found behind the boiler at the theatre was one of Bartholomew West's many sub-contractors."

"And you think ..." Lou Sphinx swallowed and then with hands which were only slightly trembling tried to fix the plastic cap back onto the polystyrene cup of coffee; the remaining faint froth still clinging to the sides.

"... that Bartholomew West really doesn't like you and he hardly ever wastes any money on going through the normal channels, or at least that's what my colleagues in Manchester and the Greater London area have told me."

"That offer of protective custody?"

"What of it?"

"Does it still stand?"

"You want to spend a night in the cells when you have your own team of private detectives looking after you?"

"Yes." Lou looked suddenly thoughtful and after a short pause stated, "And that's another thing, I think you should add another name to that list."

"Really? And who might that be?"

"Er, that retired policeman."

"Which retired policeman?"

"Bob Callow, Detective Inspector Bob Callow."

★ ★ ★

Bob yielded to Tavistock's ministrations with an ill grace bordering on rudeness.

"It's all right. Will you stop fussing, woman," he growled.

"Will you just keep still?" Tavistock snapped. "You're worse than the cat."

"The cat?" Bob exploded.

"Yes, especially if he doesn't want to be wormed." Bob swallowed and looked at her suspiciously.

"Well it will have to do but what Moira will say when you get home will probably be unrepeatable." Tavistock released Bob's head and surveyed her handiwork with antiseptic wipes and plasters with not a certain degree of pride. Bob gingerly rubbed his chin and then winced.

"Are you sure that you don't need an X-ray?" Tavistock asked.

"Positive," Bob replied, wiping another globule of blood from his nose.

"What on earth could you possibly have said to Mr Sphinx that would have made him this mad?" Tavistock asked.

"No idea," Bob lied.

Tavistock bent to pick up a cotton-wool ball, which had rolled to the side of the backstage area in which they were sitting, and touched something other than the bloodied object she had been attempting to retrieve. As her hand made contact with the small mislaid button the lights went out and the gloom which followed had her whimper in surprise.

Before her the stage and its current set of mismatched furniture and garish carpet waited patiently for the first act, the darkness punctured in places by the dull yellow glow of a dying torch. A figure stumbled from the wings and stopped as the torch played about his features.

"What the hell do you want?" the unseen holder of the light asked.

"We can't do this, Ronnie."

"Can't do what?"

"We can't pull this place down."

"And why not? It's a dump, anyone can see that, a proper dump, but to me and you and half a dozen hand-picked investors, a potential goldmine."

"But it's a theatre."

"So?"

"So it's a piece of heritage and it's unique, we can't just pull it down."

"Well no, I agree that it would have to be in a far worse condition before we did that."

"Good."

"Which is why I brought the paintstripper with me."

"Paintstripper?"

"It's an accelerant; all this is wood, so believe me when I say it will go up in no time, bit of a spark, loose wiring, somebody leaves the lid off the bottle of turps and away she goes."

"But you can't do this?"

The figure with the torch moved towards the slightly smaller man in the centre of the stage and glared down at him.

"And you will stop me how exactly?"

A soft breeze blew across the stage from the open auditorium and shadows began to creep down the wall from the Royal box festooned with flags, up the side of the orchestra pit and over the lip of the stage.

A bloodcurdling scream was ripped from the mouth of the man called Ronnie and then he was thrown to the ground by several invisible assailants, one of whom had nearly gouged out an eye with the end of his Malacca cane.

"I'll get you for this Barty, if it's the last thing I do, I'll get you for this."

Tavistock watched as a shaking Barty West ran in the direction of the stage door, stumbling as he banged into discarded flats and old barrels and boxes of props and costumes.

The stage suddenly plunged into life, spot-lit by the dozens of lights suspended above. Ronnie lay at the centre of the stage and writhed in unrestrained agony, his whole body sparkling as dust motes danced and glittered in the brilliant beams. Several voices demanded to know what Ronnie thought he was up to and as the policemen and the manager marched from various parts of the theatre to the stage, Ronnie found himself pinned to the floor by cold, invisible and exceptionally strong hands.

Tavistock looked down at the black Bakelite button in her fist and then into the staring eyes of Barty West, deceased.

"I think," she said, swallowing hard as the vision faded to be replaced by the sight of Bob struggling to sit her up, "that you had better explain what the hell that was all about."

"I think you just saw my murderer," Barty explained and then sinking to the floor with his head in his hands, he began to cry softly.

★ ★ ★

Brian Clague sat in the dimly lit booth and thoughtfully took another helping of bright red chicken, artfully sprinkled with freshly chopped virulent green coriander. Bob watched him with narrowed eyes and nibbled on a chip.

"How can you eat that stuff?" Bob asked.

"Easy, watch," Brian answered, spearing an onion bhaji with his fork.

"Does Caro know?" Bob remarked, cutting into his plain grilled steak.

"Yes she does and before you ask, no, she doesn't mind as she's gone to the cinema with one of the mothers from nursery school to see some chick flick."

"So who's minding the sprogs?"

"Dad."

"Right." Bob chased a pea around his plate and squashed it before it rolled off the edge.

"Who's minding him?"

"I have no idea, nor do I care; I have the night off, I'm eating one of my favourite meals, drinking beer and as you are my designated driver, lots of beer at that."

"Hummm, well sup up, you may need as much of this stuff as you can handle."

"All right – spill, I'm in a good mood and I'm listening."

Bob sat back and thoughtfully regarded his old partner.

"That list you had containing all the names of people who may have wanted to rid the world of Mr Sphinx?"

"What of it?"

"Did it contain the name of one Bartholomew West?"

"Yes, why?"

"The real Bartholomew West was murdered thirty-odd years ago by his then partner one Ronnie West."

"West?"

"His younger and more violent twin."

"Shades of the Krays there," Brian muttered, wiping up a patch of sauce with a Peshwari naan. "Mind you, they murdered other people not each other."

"What is that stuffed with?" Bob asked, as something white fell from the bread and landed on the food-splattered white linen tablecloth.

"Coconut and raisins," Brian remarked as he picked the crumb up with a licked finger and ate it.

"With chicken?" Bob sighed and shook his head in pained disbelief.

"I like coconut."

"So do I, but it's usually wrapped in chocolate."

"You have no soul."

"And you've got no taste buds."

A waiter passed their table and smilingly asked if everything was all right. "Splendid." Brian affirmed, reaching for the mango chutney.

Bob just grinned and took another sip of mineral water.

"I can get a taxi," Brian grunted, frowning at the water.

"Better not, I've got one of those blood tests tomorrow for my private pilot's medical and they get a bit sniffy if the old blood is forty per cent proof."

"So you're still keeping on with the flying?"

"When I can, mind you with the price of fuel what it is, who can say how long for?"

"Anyway, getting back to more mundane levels, I checked

up on Bartholomew West and according to the records across, Ronnie West died at about the same time as you said that Barty did." Brian advised, picking up a stray sultana with his thumb and index finger.

"And there was a body?" Bob asked, as he watched the delicate morsel of fruit go the way of the previous globule of coconut.

"Yes."

"And who identified it?"

"Barty ... Oh, I see ...."

"Exactly, tell me ... was this so-called brother discovered before or after the real Bartholomew West was buried in concrete?"

"Afterwards by about a week or so, difficult to tell as the body had been immersed in water for a while."

"And don't tell me ... let me guess, it was so badly disfigured that only his twin brother could identify him."

"But if it wasn't Ronnie West, who the hell was it?"

"Well either it was somebody else that our happy entrepreneur wanted rid of, or it was a convenient missing person who nobody else had claimed."

"So who would know?"

"Was he cremated?"

"Eventually when the body was released, yes."

"Convenient."

"His dying wish apparently."

"I bet it was."

Both men sat back and regarded each other with matching twisted grins.

"So who would actually know which brother was which?" Brian mused toying with his empty glass.

"Well I did have this short-lived theory that maybe the

man that initially set up their companies may have had some sort of idea, that is until I checked and discovered that the firm was started by West senior who later and most conveniently died of a surfeit of whisky and of failing to flag down a London bus."

"Failing?"

"He fell in front of it before it had time to apply the brakes; he even had the right change clutched in his hand."

"Good for him."

"Pardon?"

"They can be very funny about that sort of thing, having the wrong change; I tried to give one a fiver once, a long time ago now, got a right ticking off and told to get a taxi if I was that flush."

"And did you?"

"No, flashed my warrant card and had him metaphorically doing press-ups all the way to Marble Arch."

"Those were the days."

"Aye, we were respected then."

There was a short silence as Brian cleared the last of the metal bowls in front of him and then finally sank back into his seat, happily replete.

"I don't suppose …" Bob mused "That it wasn't an accident?"

"I could check around see if anyone still remembers something."

"A lot of water under the bridge and they might all be dead."

"I'm beginning to see too many deaths."

"So am I."

"And you are absolutely sure that the real Barty West is dead?"

"Utterly positive, have spoken to him myself ..." Bob looked up and met Brian's eyes, which were standing out on stalks.

"What's the matter now?"

"This original and best Barty West wouldn't happen to be the owner of a very rumpled suit and a truly horrendous tie, would he?" Brian asked, staring at the spare seat next to Bob.

"Possibly, why?"

"Well either I've had far too much to drink or he just winked at me."

"Is he still there?"

"Er, yes."

"Then ask him why his younger brother Kiki West didn't spill the beans, after all he or indeed she must have been able to tell them apart."

Barty West scratched an ear and then shrugged. "He was only a baby when I died, the old man got frisky in Blackpool one night, Mum must have thought she was past having another kid and a minor miracle happened; perhaps he was too young to notice any difference between us."

"But your mother?" Brian prompted.

"Died in childbirth, Dad never got over it; that's why the bus thing made sense."

"Right."

"Er, whose mother?" Bob asked, leaning across the table.

"Barty's, she died in childbirth, which is why Kiki ..."

"Kirk."

"Pardon?" Bob and Brian asked in unison but to different questions.

Barty sighed.

"My little brother was called Kirk, after Kirk Douglas

but he changed it to Kiki when he got the biological extras."

"Why can't Bob see you?" Brian whispered as Bob vainly squinted at the place where Barty sat.

"Because he isn't to be my instrument of justice," Barty answered and then vanished abruptly just as the waiter returned to ask them whether they wanted any coffee.

* * *

Ronnie West stood silently in the gathering gloom of the boiler room and scowled. Tangled memories and thoughts, which he hadn't given house room to for very many years, wandered uninvited through his head.

The space in which the hired help had been shoved was smaller than he'd imagined.

"Not enough room to squeeze a cat," he mused aloud.

"Although plenty of room still for a snake," a voice behind him purred.

"Oh, it's you." Ronnie groaned disdainfully. "I should have known."

"You used to pinch my toys and then break them," the voice accused, moving silently towards him.

"Little boys shouldn't play with dolls."

"But they were my dolls," the voice mused.

There was a short pause broken by Ronnie lighting a cigarette. The aroma of strong tobacco wafted up and into the exposed rafters.

"You shouldn't smoke that, you know."

"So sue me."

"Or at least not down here, too many flammable substances, but then I guess you already know that." The voice then gave vent to a laugh of genuine amusement.

"Poor old Barty, he really liked this place, didn't he? Too much to let you burn it to the ground, I wonder …"

"What?"

"Is that why you killed him?"

Ronnie West turned abruptly on his accuser and glared into a pair of clear blue eyes ringed in kohl. "One word, just one and you're a dead man."

"Man?" The eyes widened and a pair of carmine lips pursed in theatrical petulance. "Man." The words were laced with amusement, "I haven't been a man since you sodomised me, or can't you remember that small pleasure?"

"What do you want?" Ronnie demanded, turning away.

"You can turn your back on me as many times as you like, brother dearest, but rumour has it that you are running out of time and alibis. So few good deeds in a naughty world and in your case absolutely no good deeds at all."

"Have you come here simply to talk me to death or did you actually want something?" Ronnie extracted a wad of cash from a jacket pocket and began to count the notes. "I have a thousand in used fifties; will that do for now? You can have a cheque for the rest."

"Funnily enough I don't want money, not this time."

"Then what the hell do you want? Kirk, Kiki, or whatever hell name you're using now."

Kiki walked towards the large green boiler which loomed in front of them.

"I want it all to stop and, brother dear, I want to see you get what you really and truly deserve."

"And what might that be, you little insignificant bastard?" Ronnie hissed.

"Oh no, I can't possibly tell, it would spoil all our fun," Kirk laughed and then almost appeared to vanish into the shadows of the surrounding wall.

Ronnie marched to the back of the room, realising far too late that there was nobody there.

“Our?” he shouted, “Our? What the hell do you mean our?”

Above him in one of the dressing rooms the three conspirators toasted their forthcoming success and played the tape back, again.

Chapter Ten

Bartholomew West braced himself against the side of the fishing boat currently taking him out to sea and turned towards the youth in the jeans and black hoodie.

"I did what you asked me to, Mr West sir, the virus worked well good, everything will be slowly nibbled away and they won't be able to get any of the data back and even if they do it will be garbled beyond recognition."

"Good, good," Bartholomew West chuckled as he reached into an inner pocket.

"So when do I get the rest of what's owed me?" The acned youth asked, leaning forward, the metal studs in his eyebrows and nose bobbing furiously with the swell of the boat.

"Oh, about now," Bartholomew advised, moving nearer until they were almost chest to chest. There was a muffled bang, the youth's eyes opened wide and then looked faintly puzzled as he felt something warm and sticky running down the inside of his cotton top.

Bartholomew West took a step back and began to wipe the nozzle of the handgun he still held in one of his pockets with a cotton handkerchief. The fisherman who had been up to that point quietly cutting up fish and throwing the bits into a large plastic bin looked up and almost smiled.

"Mr Haslet, I want you to get rid of this particular body in such a way that no one ever finds any of it," Bartholomew barked as the indistinct shape of Castle Rushen loomed at them out of the encroaching sea mist.

The fisherman smiled knowingly and moved unhurriedly towards the wheelhouse.

"Kenny, we need to go out past the Chicken Rock after we drop Mr West off at Fort Island and I'll be needing the big chainsaw."

Bartholomew West stood twenty minutes later surrounded by sea thrift and squabbling seabirds on dry ground and stretched, yawning. His old Land Rover stood in a corner of the car park, a solitary rusting vehicle surrounded by grasping fingers of meandering fog.

Bartholomew could, if he strained both ears, still hear the gentle putt, putt of the fishing boat's engines as it struggled against the tide and picked its way carefully through the jagged granite rocks and out to deeper safer water.

* * *

Marianna looked up at the wall and smirked broadly, the lines on her face creasing in appreciative mirth.

"I'm so glad you find it so very amusing," a deep male voice beside her whispered nastily.

Marianna turned slowly and fixed the casually dressed figure of Lou Sphinx with a tight smile.

"Oh, God!" Lou exclaimed. "You!"

"I know, my sweet, of all the theatres in all the land you

have to pick this one to turn up in and bore the pants off everyone," Marianna replied.

"You didn't?" Lou asked, pointing at the still dripping graffiti.

"No, but I think the sentiments are admirable," Marianna cooed.

"You too?" Lou moaned. "Why the hell does everyone hate me?" he complained, sticking his hands deep into the pockets of his baggy scarlet corduroy trousers.

"Oh I don't know ..." Marianna mused, "perhaps it's simply because you're a lying, scheming, two-timing piece of shit?"

"I never two-timed you," Lou spluttered.

"No?"

"No."

"Really, then what do you call swanning off with my best friend then?"

"I left a note explaining everything."

"A note! You left me at the altar of our church with our friends and you left a sodding note!" Marianna exploded and then hit him hard in the face with the flat of her hand. Lou taken completely unawares, recoiled and fell against the wall.

"I guess I might have deserved that," he gasped, his eyes still watering.

"Oh, be still my beating heart, a celeb being bitch slapped and it isn't even the end of the week, lucky me," Geoff chuckled as he passed both antagonists.

"Oh piss off, Geoff," Marianna hissed.

"Yeah, piss off," Lou agreed, gingerly rubbing the side of his face.

"That hurt," he hissed as Geoff wandered off gaily

whistling something vaguely familiar to them both from the Mikado.

"It was meant to and I should have done it years ago," Marianna crushingly advised him.

"How … I mean …" Lou straightened himself up and after taking a deep breath muttered, "I was sorry to hear about the … the … baby." His voice tailed away and he looked if anything older and somehow smaller.

"Thanks," Marianna snarled. "You could have written."

"I thought about it."

"Thought about it?"

"Just didn't think it would do any good."

"Just water under the bridge, time the great healer and other crap banalities, eh?" Marianna scoffed.

"Something like that."

"My Dad was all for hiring someone to put you in a short coffin."

"Really? Er … why a short coffin?"

"What? Oh, because he wanted to cut your legs off at your privates first before he administered the *coup de grâce*, whatever; however in the end and after he'd sobered up, he decided that it would just be a complete waste of money."

"Right."

"Frankly my dear, most people really don't give a damm!" Marianna drawled.

Lou Sphinx regarded her in an uneasy fashion and then once more turned his attention to the defaced surface in front of them both.

"So somebody wants to kill you even more badly than I did once?" Marianna observed looking again at the blood-red letters scrawled across the corridor wall.

"Someone always does," Lou sighed.

"Tell me sweetie, as I'm really dying to find out, but apart from the weekly death threats, are you happy?" Marianna asked.

"No, not particularly, no." Lou replied with feeling.

"Good, that's all I actually needed to know." Marianna laughed and then patted him very gently on the side of the face, just about where she'd slapped him. "You see darling, after you left me and when I'd actually come to my senses I realised how very miserable we would actually have been."

"Right."

Marianna smiled sweetly up at him and then, still laughing, sauntered off towards her dressing room. Lou stayed and silently watched her ample form saunter off, her high-heeled bejewelled shoes clicking rhythmically in time to her swaying buttocks.

"And if we had stayed together, my love, I actually think that it would have made me very happy indeed," Lou whispered to the empty hallway.

* * *

Jemima Banks sat at her husband's bedside and surveyed his pale face with an expression of pity mixed with not a little anger.

Tony Banks woke suddenly and on seeing who was watching him smiled beatifically, a smile short-lived as Brian Clague and Bob Callow moved from the doorway, where they had been chatting to several members of the nursing staff, back towards his bed.

"Feeling a bit better now?" Brian asked, sitting on the only other available chair. Bob, looking around for another and finding none, lolled against a convenient wall and folded his arms across his ample chest.

"Er, yes thanks," Tony answered, watching Bob Callow out of the corner of his eye.

"Take no notice of old Bob there, he's retired."

"Really? He doesn't look that retired to me," Tony answered, a querulous note in his voice.

"He's really only here because I'm using him in a consultancy role, sort of thing," Brian smiled.

"And I found you under the stage probably dying and I'm almost pathologically nosy," Bob smirked.

"Right, I think," Tony mumbled and then sat up as he remembered something else.

"What happened to the lady that found me she wasn't … wasn't …"

"A ghost?" Bob chuckled.

"Er, yes."

"No, she was – and still is – alive and kicking."

"Oh good, only …"

"A lot of people you've met recently have been dead," Brian growled, daring Bob to say anything. Jemima looked from one to the other in astonishment and wondered if someone had been a bit too free with the medication.

"So tell me, Mr Banks, what do you know about a Bartholomew West?"

"Well, I set his companies up after his father and brother died."

"His brother Ronnie West?"

"Yes."

"And did you ever meet this Ronnie West?"

"I don't think … hang on: I did I saw them both, just the once and very briefly. It was about a day before they put in a bid for the theatre … they wanted to draw up a few documents and contracts."

"Them, you met them both?" Bob asked, suddenly very interested.

"Yes."

"And what were they like?"

"Well I … it's difficult to tell really … I mean they were twins for a start, almost identical, and they had the same sort of mannerisms but …"

"What?"

"I always got the feeling that Barty was frightened of his brother and that Ronnie was not quite all there, I mean he wasn't mad or anything he was just, well … hard."

"Hard?"

"In the way that granite is."

"And you met them only briefly; how briefly?"

"Just a handshake really, it was my old boss who set everything up, poor man; he retired about a week later and then had an accident shortly afterwards."

"An accident?"

"Some sort of boating accident in the Lake District, it was all very sudden and very sad."

"And would you have been able to tell one West brother from another?"

"No. Mind you I was a bit alarmed when Ronnie was arrested by the police for trying to burn down the theatre," Tony mused, remembering. "Now that is odd …"

"What?"

"He got the duty advocate to get him released. I mean, none of the West family ever took legal aid, they always said that you never knew who you were getting, they preferred to always pay, you see …"

"And that one instant they didn't?"

"No, and I was waiting for the call, I waited all night,

even stayed in the office, then of course Ronnie absconded and there was the accident."

"Another watery demise," Brian prompted.

"Yes … actually, now I come to think about it there were an awful lot of accidents that year."

"Especially in that particular family," Bob grunted.

"I don't suppose you ever had any suspicion that Barty may actually have been his brother Ronnie?"

"No I don't … I mean I didn't. Hang on, there was an incident … something involving one of the secretaries … some sort of inappropriate remark or remarks … I think I jokingly told Mr West that his behaviour was more like his late brother's."

"And did he ever behave like that again?" Brian asked, making a few notes.

"Actually no … now I come to think of it … in fact after that I always either met him in a restaurant or in his office."

Brian and Bob shared a knowing look and then Brian dropped his bombshell.

"The thing is, Tony, that we think that Ronnie murdered the real Barty West in a hotel cellar thirty years ago and then stole his identity, faked his own death and has perpetrated numerous other felonies since."

"What!"

"In fact he is, we think, the one who threatened you and your family."

"But why? I mean there are still all the old company records."

"No, not now there isn't because according to your office the records held on computer for both your firm and that of Mr West's accountant have been attacked by some sort of a virus hidden in an email purporting to have come from Manxnet."

"All of it? But what about the old records?"

"Last night someone got into the storage facility where such records are kept and started a fire. Nothing, I'm afraid, could be salvaged."

Jemima leant towards her stricken husband, all anger dissipated as she began to realise the full enormity of her husband's game of hide and seek.

"He was really going to kill me, wasn't he?" Tony whispered.

"We think so, yes; initially we think that he just wanted to scare you into silence long enough for him to incriminate you and liquidate most of his assets and leave the country, but at some point that changed and he set out to do a more permanent job on containing you."

"But now that you've found Tony, what's to stop him doing it again?" Jemima asked.

"Nothing, except for the fact that we will give out the sad news that Tony is in a coma and not expected to live and that the police are still baffled as to why he was living in the Gaiety Theatre," Brian reassured her with a grin before adding, "Anyway, Bob here has a cunning plan and we have every faith in the fact that an arrest is very imminent."

"First nights – don't you just love 'em?" Bob chuckled.

Brian gave Bob a brief nod, and after assuring both Tony and Jemima of his protection, left to brief the rest of his team on the more recent and more believable developments. Bob sauntered away from the main hospital clutching a freshly made sandwich, a cup of takeaway coffee and a slab of cake intent on finding both Tavistock and Mannanan at the one place he knew they would be staking out, the Gaiety Theatre.

Tony clutched his wife's hand and relaxed for the first time in days.

"You do know that I have to go back and help, don't you?" he asked after a while.

"Oh yes, I know and if I can I'll help too," Jemima assured him with a wry smile.

Tony leant towards her and gave her proffered lips a brief kiss.

"Tony?"

"Yes, love?"

"I suppose we'll have to give it back …"

"Give what back?"

"The five hundred thousand pounds."

"The what!"

Tony stared at his wife in utter disbelief. "What five hundred thousand?"

* * *

Russell regarded the debonair and immaculately suited figure of Richard Allan, the current reincarnation of a Victorian director, with a deep sense of foreboding and sighed, whilst at the same moment wishing for the fifth time that morning that he had just thrown the alarm clock at the nearest wall, turned over and gone back to sleep.

"I don't really care what you think, Russell, but that blasted jester of yours has gone too far this time."

"Now look here, Richard old chap, as I keep trying to tell you ad nauseum, the Phantom is still in hospital …"

"And then I bloody well hope they lock him up and throw away the key …"

"... and so could not possibly have committed the heinous crime of which he is now accused." Russell paused for breath and glared back at him. "By the way just as a matter of interest what has the poor demented fool supposedly done now, stolen somebody else's lunch, nicked the props, or heaven forbid moved one of the flats?"

"He's scrawled, 'Ill get you yet you bastard' across the wall next to the lower dressing rooms, and my cast are understandably upset, especially Stella, who as you know is of a nervous enough disposition already without that sort of bad language," Richard replied, before adding, "Although even I have to admit that once she gets on stage she's absolutely splendid, a true trooper, even when she put that nail through her foot she carried on regardless and she only fainted after the last curtain call."

"Wrote on the wall!" Russell repeated, almost speechless with rage.

"In red paint," Richard replied and then added, "gloss," as a well-timed final insult.

"Graffiti on my wall!" Russell stood up, metaphoric steam erupting from both ears.

"It could have been worse, you know," Richard mused.

"How could it possibly be worse than red gloss paint? That's oil-based you know."

"Whoever it was could have done it somewhere in the auditorium, the main entrance or even dare I say it the Matcham Suite. The possible permutations are indeed endless."

Russell ground his teeth and rose abruptly from behind his desk; Richard startled took a step back and collided noisily with a temporarily parked filing cabinet.

"I quite frankly couldn't care less if they wrote the entire first half of the book of Genesis on that wretched paper they insisted on using, but those corridors have only just been finished and you wouldn't believe the hoops I had to dance through to get the works department to actually turn up and do it."

Russell stormed from his office and headed off for the backstage area where a collection of interested staff, partially clad members of the cast and persons with nothing better to do were discussing the recent artwork.

"Someone needs to get a dictionary," one wag exclaimed, "he's left out the apostrophe on 'I'll'."

"*I'll* bring it up at the next management meeting, shall I?" Russell interjected. Heads turned in his direction and then there was a general hurried disbursement of bodies, as each decided they had better things to do than to be the whipping boy of a gently smoking theatre manager.

"Red gloss," Richard reiterated from behind him.

"I can see that," Russell snarled

"Our red gloss and we barely had enough for the doors as it was."

"Richard?"

"Yes Russell?"

"Bugger off."

"Oh right, just thought you ought to know, perhaps notify that detective that is always hanging around."

"Why?"

"Just in case it has something to do with that reality television thingy chap."

"Ah, you mean …"

"That if it was meant for him they could cough up a tenner or so for some more paint."

Russell turned and fixed him with a look that would have

had the nearest Samurai falling on his sword and then apologising for the mess as he did so.

"I'll, er, just go and see a man about a … a … more paint then."

Richard hastened off down the starkly lit corridor and vanished abruptly as he tramped up the stairs to the upper dressing rooms.

Russell stood and stared at the blood-red still dripping words until he was joined by the ample and gently puffing figure of Bob Callow.

"Am I to assume that your hospital vigil is over?" Russell asked.

"Yes. And not a moment too soon from the look of this," Bob remarked, touching a sticky dribble with his finger.

"Still wet and recently done by a poor speller who wasn't, I presume, seen by anyone," Bob asserted almost gleefully.

"A rough but unfortunately correct assumption," Russell ruefully agreed, turning away from the wall in question. "I don't suppose you could advise Mr Sphinx that he ought to leave my … er … this theatre for the good of his health?"

"I really don't think that he would take any notice of anything I had to say at all." Bob gingerly rubbed at the bruised skin under one eye and grinned.

"I see." Russell took a deep breath and then, decision made, stalked off towards the stage.

A few minutes later he stood alone in the props room and shouted "Rupert!"

"You yelled?" Rupert exclaimed, materialising in front of him.

"This has got to stop. I want you to find the perpetrator of this most recent piece of gross vandalism and then I want you to bring him or her to me, and I really don't care how you go about it."

"And if we can't?"

"Then I shall allow a televised exorcism of this theatre."

"What!"

"It's you or them, take your choice. I'm going out for a very liquid lunch and when I stagger back I want a result." Russell glared at the poleaxed spook in front of him and smiling, in as unpleasant a fashion as he could muster, he left.

Rupert regarded the space which Russell had briefly occupied in stunned silence. Gradually the room filled with curious spirits, including the lady in black and a gaggle of dancers.

"I don't suppose anybody would like to volunteer to tell Russell something?"

There was a short silence into which Mad Harry appeared, dragging a reluctant Mervin clutching an empty paint can.

"Are you going to tell them or shall I?" Mad Harry barked, thrusting the unfortunate entity into the centre of the room.

"Tell him what?" Mannanan demanded as he slowly materialised amongst the coagulating dust.

"How long have you been there?" Rupert demanded.

"Long enough," Mannanan answered, regarding Mad Harry with a thoughtful expression.

"Your friend is well on the way to recovery and has finally been reunited with his wife and children."

"And his wife is speaking to him?" Mad Harry asked.

"Just about, but there were definite whiffs of rising sulphur when I left his bedside."

"Ah well, c'est la vie, as they say in frogland."

"You do realise how politically incorrect that phrase is?" Rupert barked.

"I'm dead, so who the hell cares? Speaking of which, what do we do about Russell?" Mad Harry enquired, thoughtfully eyeing the door, which an irate Russell had slammed shut in passing.

"He'll get over it," Rupert replied, twiddling his cane in a nervous fashion.

"Well, I'm not so sure, and after listening to young Mervin here I'm not convinced that you will be either," Mad Harry hissed.

All eyes turned as one to stare at Mervin who was trying to back away into a wall but was hampered in his efforts by the appearance of Barty West and the reappearance of Russell who both stood solidly behind him.

Mannanan glanced briefly in Barty's direction and then glared directly at him.

"What are you wearing?" he demanded.

"It's a T-shirt; I got fed up with the suit so I thought I'd go for a new and younger look."

"What is that, that thing?" Mannanan growled, pointing at the centre of the offending garment.

"It's a frog," Barty answered.

"It's a frog with a … a …" One of the dancers fainted.

"It's called 'the annoying thing'," Barty advised the interested onlookers.

"Most appropriate," Russell muttered, before adding, "not that I usually would condone such attire but in the current circumstances …"

"Quite," Mannanan barked.

"I like it, it goes with the shorts," Barty sniffed.

"Shorts?" Mad Harry regarded him for a brief moment

and nearly muttered a very rude word; fortunately Mervin had regained his attention by trying to ooze through the nearby door in a furtive attempt to regain the safety of the boiler room.

"Oh no you don't!" Mad Harry shouted, grabbing Mervin by what was generally considered the scruff of the neck and hauling him back.

"I want you to tell everyone here just exactly what you saw the other day and last night and then we can decide how to get out of this almighty mess."

Mervin swallowed noisily and then in a muted falsetto squeak began, "I saw this big chap hiding in the shadows; I was going to throw something at him when I noticed Mad Harry behind him."

"So what did you do?" Rupert asked.

"Nothing, I thought Harry would save me the bother," Mervin gulped and then added, "Which he did, he said 'Boo' really loudly and this big bloke just toppled over, right there in front of him. Harry looked dead surprised, he was really funny, so I laughed and Harry said that if I told anyone he'd rip my head from my body and feed it to the gulls."

"Charming," Rupert interjected.

"And then Harry vanished, he was only gone like a minute or so and this other bloke turned up and he was carrying something, it looked a bit like a rounders bat, anyway I saw him wander over to the body and turn it over and then he made this funny gasping sound and he kept muttering that you couldn't trust anyone to do anything properly and then he pulled the bloke that Harry had killed …"

"How was I to know that he had a dodgy ticker?" Harry demanded crossly.

"… and stuffed him behind the boiler; he had to break a

few things first though 'cos I heard the bones snap when he hit them with the bat thing, and then he wiped all his prints off everything and he just went."

"I don't suppose you recognised who he was?"

"Oh yes I did, and that was the funny thing, it's why I thought I ought to tell Harry."

"Well go on then, tell him," Mannanan prompted.

"It was that bloke, the one that tried to burn the theatre down, you remember, just before it was sold to the Government. The bloke we caught and kept from running away so that the police could arrest him. It was years back, you must know him, he tried to kill you." Mervin turned towards Barty who was staring at him in disbelief.

"Ronnie?"

"Well he calls himself Barty now, and that's not all either, last night I heard him being blackmailed by this woman, or at least I thought it was a she, only Ronnie called her his little brother, which made no sense at all. But I do know one thing."

"What?"

"She was the one that wrote on the wall this morning and the funny thing is that she had help …" Everyone looked at him and then one of the dancers for whom the excitement was becoming all too much shouted, "Well go on then, tell us!"

"… from Mr Sphinx, so what I wanted to know was, why would he make a threat against himself?"

"Are you sure?" Russell asked, frowning.

"Oh yes, positive. He held the paint and that assistant of his, the one that he's always snapping at and making cry, she was holding the torch, and this is the most interesting bit, she called him darling and then when they'd finished they had a quick snog in the corner," Mervin giggled.

"But I thought that she hated him?" Russell interjected with a frown, remembering the most recent incident when he'd had to resort to the good gin to calm her frayed nerves.

"Not the mousy one in the cardigan and the droopy hem?" Rupert spluttered.

"Yes her, and when I saw her she was anything but retiring," Mervin grinned broadly as he remembered some of the finer and more energetic details. "And I'll tell you one thing, I didn't know you could do that sort of thing with a mop head and a broom handle."

"Mervin, there are ladies present," Edwin interrupted as he attempted to cover Gloria's ears.

"Oh shut up," the old lady in black croaked as she sidled in Mervin's direction. "Some of us who had lives would like to know." There was a chorus of 'Yeses' from the dancers and Mervin had the grace to blush.

"I couldn't say any more it was a bit, you know, personal but if you really want all the gory details I'll tell you all later, downstairs," and with that he vanished, swiftly followed by the female members of the ghost fraternity and quite a few males.

Mannanan regarded Barty in a thoughtful fashion.

"I presume that this aforementioned arsonist is your psychotic brother and is also the person that hit you over the back of the head and buried you in concrete?"

"You left out the bit where he pushed my old man under a train, abused my younger brother and pinched my building firm."

"And this is the man we are supposed to be saving?" Mannanan grumbled and again looked at his clipboard. "Although he isn't actually down here."

"So maybe we could just wait and see what happens," Barty muttered hopefully.

"Well, don't expect any of us to help, as far as I'm concerned it was a great pity that Mad Harry was prevented from tearing him limb from limb the last time," Rupert asserted, looking mutinously around at the remaining ghosts who all nodded vigorously in agreement.

"And will you all stop with the Mad, the name is Harry. I'm as sane as the rest of you, I just have a problem with anger management, that's all."

"Anger management?" Russell reiterated cautiously.

"I've talked it over with a friend of mine and he's getting me one of those self-help books."

"Self-help?" Rupert repeated, an incredulous note in his normally calm voice.

"When he gets out of hospital, that is."

"And when he finishes helping the police with their current enquiries," Mannanan prompted.

"And if the missus hasn't killed him," Barty added in carefully neutral tones.

"Well, all right, I might not get it immediately, but I'm trying to take a step back and consult my inner self before I do anything," Harry grunted.

"I thought that's what you always did, hence the title mad," Russell remarked.

Harry glared at him and then taking a deep and very loud breath, counted slowly up to ten in perfect German before replying. "Anyway, I think our real problem is one of loyalties and ultimately what is best for this theatre."

"Now there I am in total agreement with Ma … er, our friend Harry," Rupert announced. There was more nodding until everyone was regarding Russell with equally bated breath.

"Don't look at me, I have no idea what to do, that's why I'm here."

"I think that I might have thought of a solution beneficial to all," Mannanan pondered, looking around until he had everyone's attention.

"But are we going to like it?" Rupert asked.

"That all depends on whether or not you can all follow instructions," Mannanan replied as he stalked from the room, Barty hurrying in his wake.

"What are you all looking at me for?" Harry grumbled.

"No reason, no reason at all," Rupert answered thoughtfully, before turning to regard the closed door through which Mannanan had walked.

"I just hope that whatever the big man has decided doesn't involve a complete renovation of the auditorium."

"What!" Russell exclaimed.

"I mean to say, that rumour about rearranging an entire cliff-face, totally and utterly true." Russell's face went a pale shade of green and he collapsed into a nearby chair which had been thoughtfully pulled towards him by Cecil, who was really beginning to enjoy himself.

"But I'm sure he won't do anything quite that drastic, perhaps just a gentle decorating job and let's face it, you've never really liked that new wallpaper," Cecil remarked as he patted him kindly on the shoulder.

* * *

Tavistock looked at the crumpled tearstained face of her youngest child and rolled her eyes.

"All right, out with it, what did you do with the tail?"

Emily opened one clenched fist and revealed a long bedraggled piece of string with what looked like a cotton-wool ball on the end.

"Kate is going to kill you, you do know that, don't you?"

"Yes mum."

"Have you any idea what it actually looked like before you borrowed it?" Tavistock asked, handling the soggy saturated object with great care.

"It looked like the picture in the book."

"Right," Tavistock muttered, and turning, regarded the closed door of her eldest daughter's bedroom with an air of dread. She knocked and then waited.

"Go away," something shouted.

"Do you have that book, the one with your costume in it?" Tavistock asked the disinterested wooden barrier.

"Yes."

"Well can I have it just for a moment?"

"Why?"

"Because I want to."

"Oh." There was the sound of scrabbling and of objects being pushed across the floor. Finally the door opened a fraction and a large artist's sketchbook was pushed through the narrow aperture. "I want it back after tea," Kate announced and then after about a second added. "What is for tea?"

"Spag bog."

"Great."

The door was pushed shut and the mobile disco resumed at a slightly louder level.

Tavistock clutched the book and hurried down the stairs and into the kitchen, where she opened the pages at a set of costumes, enthusiastically designed by her eldest daughter for the school's end-of-term fashion show. She then looked again at the dripping tangle of fur, wool and limp sequins. The original sketch showed a bejewelled and spangled she-devil complete with a red satin basque, tulle skirt, which looked suspiciously like a puff ball skirt she'd bought in the eighties and had only had the courage to wear once, and a long elegant forked tail, the remnants of which now lay in a pitifully sparse mess on a piece of newspaper, placed carefully on the table by a helpful Emily. Tavistock sniffed.

"Where did you get the paper from?" she asked.

"Under the cat's bowl." Emily replied. "I thought it would help dry it out, 'cos of when you stuff our shoes with paper when we've been down the beach."

"Emily?"

"Yes."

"Why don't you go and watch Sponge Bob or Zoë 101 or something?"

"Can't."

"Why not?"

"'Cos they aren't on."

"What is on."

"'My Parents are Aliens'."

"I wish I was," Tavistock muttered, picking out a large piece of cat food and several smaller biscuits from the pink mess of slowly congealing fibres.

"Emily, why don't you go and watch that then before mummy puts you in the washing machine as well as your sister's art project?"

Emily took one look at her mother's face and raced off to the lounge.

Tavistock tipped some dried pasta in a boiling pan of

water and went back to staring at the disaster on the table.

"What was it?" Mannanan asked emerging from the kitchen wall.

"It was supposed to be that ..." Tavistock replied, pointing to the bright and garish drawing in Kate's art book, '... until Emily borrowed it to show her friend for some strange and logical reason, which could only make some sort of sense if you are ten, she then put it in her jeans pocket, promptly forgot that it was there and I washed it. Well, I've managed to wash George's mobile phone and Richards's Lottery ticket so a sequinned tail is a bit of a doddle really. Restoring it to its original form may not be so easy."

Mannanan gave it a gentle prod and then, leaning over, sniffed.

"Why does it smell of fish?" he asked.

"Long story involving a helpful Emily."

"What would you do if I could fix this and restore it to its original form?"

"Anything you wanted, short of jumping out of a cake in black suspenders and a tasselled bra."

"Really?"

"Really."

"Don't look."

"Wouldn't dream of it." Tavistock closed her eyes and waited.

A few minutes later Mannanan prodded her on the shoulder. "You can look now."

Tavistock did and couldn't believe her eyes; the tail glittered in all of its original scarlet silken glory and looked not dissimilar to the stylised drawing.

"How on earth ... no don't tell me just let me go and restore this to number one daughter and then I am going to give you a big sqelchy hug."

Minutes later she was back and grinning happily.

"Mission accomplished?" Mannanan asked. "Only I think something is burning."

Tavistock swore and just managed to fish the casserole dish of Bolognese sauce from the oven before the chargrilled mess of meat and tomato welded itself to the bottom of the pan.

"So what do you want?" Tavistock asked, looking into the depths of the pot.

"Well, luckily it wasn't dinner," Mannanan answered.

"I think I may just ring up the Chinese restaurant on the corner."

"Good idea. I'll take the saucepan of pasta off the heat, shall I?"

"Er, yes please." Tavistock switched the oven off and began to search in one of the kitchen drawers for the takeaway menu.

"How would you like to be instrumental in restoring justice to a sorry world?" Mannanan asked.

"As long as I don't have to pay anything, I'm all for it, why?"

"I – no – we, need your help."

"My help?"

"I would like you to do your psychic bit down at the Gaiety Theatre."

"Oh?"

"Actually what I would like you to do is to help me set up Ronnie West our multiple murderer, by denouncing him in public and on stage."

"And this will help how?"

"Well if we set it up properly he'll finally crack and

hopefully we'll get it all on film."

"Why ask me? Why not get Lou Sphinx to do it?"

"Because you can actually see real ghosts and because Ronnie has never met you and with any luck won't even know who you are if somebody mentions your name."

"But ..."

"Apart from which, he won't, for reasons I really don't have time to go into, believe Mr Sphinx, but he will swallow every word you say."

"He will?"

"Oh yes, and before I go I ought to give this to you."

"What on earth is it?" Tavistock stared at the thin book that Mannanan had thrust into her hands with a puzzled frown.

"It's a script."

"For what?"

"'Blithe Spirit' by Noel Coward."

"Look Buster, I can see that, I've had to prompt the bloody thing often enough recently. What I can't see is why I have to have it?"

"Because you are going to play the part of Madame Arcati on opening night, the night of Midsummer's Eve, the night when Lou Sphinx is filming at the theatre, the night when the great and the good have all been invited for a gala performance, including one of the sponsors, a certain Bartholomew West of West Investments and Entertainments plc."

"But I can't possibly learn all of this!"

"You won't have to, all you have to do is remember the scene with the seance, the rest will be up to me and my team."

"Your team?"

"Let's just say that the special effects for this one performance will be really spectacular."

Chapter Eleven

Kiki West looked down into her almost empty pint glass and sighed long and deeply. She was tired, she was miserable and the big gamble she had banked upon had borne no fruit whatsoever.

Lou Sphinx sat beside her and regarded his vodka with a splash of tonic in uncharacteristic silence.

Cheryl his pseudo-assistant muttered, "Same again, lads?" and staggered off to the bar, where the barman glared at her and finally and extremely grudgingly prepared another round of drinks.

Tavistock, who had entered the Glue Pot from the swing-bridge side, looked around the crowded room and spotting her quarry, pounced before they could think up a suitable excuse and leave.

"Budge up," she hissed, looking towards the bar and spotting the barman who she vaguely knew, mouthed 'Gin and slim' and then added a thumbs-up salute when he nodded and added it to Cheryl's already laden tray.

"Who the hell are you?" Kiki asked, tossing back a

blonde lock of hair in irritation.

"Tavistock Allan."

"Ah, a writer," Lou muttered and then added, "which would explain a lot of things including the earrings."

"What's wrong with them?"

"I've seen smaller table lamps," Lou grumbled. "Where the hell are those drinks?"

"Here they are, now keep your shirt on," Cheryl snapped at him.

"What do you want?" Cheryl added as she passed Tavistock her gin.

"I'd like to win the Booker ..."

Lou snorted noisily into his drink.

"... But I'll settle for helping you to incarcerate Ronnie West," she replied.

"Ronnie West is dead; he's also my brother, which is how I know that he's dead," Kiki remarked, watching her from black-rimmed eyes.

"No, Ronnie is alive and kicking; Barty West has just been exhumed from his cement coffin and you three are trying your hand at a little blackmail and attempted murder."

All three listeners stopped drinking and went completely still.

"Or you would be if some bugger hadn't found your carefully smuggled and concealed weapon of choice," Tavistock informed them as she carefully removed the lemon wedge from her drink and nibbled at the thick yellow peel. There was a stunned silence.

"Well?" Tavistock asked. "Did I leave anything out?"

"I didn't know that that poor man was hiding in the theatre and would steal those sandwiches; I certainly didn't think that he'd eat them all," Cheryl stated, looking nervously at her drink.

"And the ground glass in the vodka?" Tavistock asked, poking an ice cube with her index finger.

"How on earth was I supposed to know that the cleaner would drink it?" Lou growled. "It's not my fault if the staff indulge in a spot of alcoholic larceny is it?"

"You really are a rather nasty little man, aren't you?" Tavistock asserted, glaring at him. Lou tried to hold eye contact, failed and resorted to opening a packet of peanuts with his teeth.

At that point two returning sailors erupted into the small confines of the snug and raucously demanded food and drink from someone called Larry who was hiding in the bowels of the pub.

"Look lady, in case you don't know a hint when you get one ..." Lou leant forwards and looking her directly in the eyes, hissed, "Piss off." He then sat back on his uncomfortable wooden bench seat and waited for her outraged reaction.

Tavistock grinned back at him and whispered "No," before leaning nonchalantly against the wall behind her seat and examining each of the conspirators in turn. After gaining their full and collective attention she cradled her gin and tonic in both hands and grinned knowingly. "Let's just say, for argument's sake, that if you were to turn up on the opening night of 'Blithe Spirit' with a camera crew that I and my associates could get Ronnie to confess to the murder of his twin brother, Barty West."

"And how the hell are you going to do that?" Lou exploded.

"Because unlike you I can actually really commune with

the dead." Tavistock replied matter of factly.

"Prove it." Kiki demanded.

"You want me to prove it?" Tavistock repeated.

All three listeners nodded and the silently watching Barty West smiled broadly and rubbed his hands.

"All right then, let me see ..." she closed her eyes and sat back, Barty moved closer and as he did the three conspirators shivered.

"What do you want to know, Kirk?" she asked, opening her eyes and focusing on him.

"The name's Kiki," Kiki muttered, wrapping her cardigan around her.

"It used to be Kirk, and he was a right little sod, tell him that I still remember the toothpaste in the slippers and if he thought that I had really fallen for the idea that the dog had taken the Swiss chocolates from my bedside table he's more of a plonker than that idiot Shane," Barty advised, moving a glass carefully to the very centre of the table.

Kiki watched the glass in mounting horror. "How the hell did you do that?" She asked.

"I didn't," Tavistock answered, "Barty did, he also said that you put toothpaste in his slippers, had a penchant for Swiss chocolate and a friend called Shane."

"Shit," Kiki whispered, glancing nervously around.

"How very theatrical," Lou scoffed. "But tell us something that will frighten Ronnie so badly that he'll loose that famous calm."

"Well, firstly you could say that you had seen him stuff the body found in the theatre behind the boiler, which by the way he did but you didn't really see."

"I can do that," Lou shrugged.

"And you, Kiki, can travel up in the Corsican Trap and

with a little make-up and a bad suit can look exactly like your brother Barty did right up to the point when Ronnie whacked him over the back of the head with a spade."

"I was told that he'd drowned."

"Well I guess that technically he did as they found concrete in his lungs."

"I meant in water," Kiki muttered, going a pale grey colour.

"That's absolutely horrible," Cheryl whimpered, swallowing hard.

"It wasn't much fun for Barty either," Tavistock remarked, taking a sip of gin.

"But how will that make him confess? He'll just see it as part of the show and anyway what's so special about the Corsican Trap, as you call it?" Kiki asked.

"It lifts one person from under the stage in such a way that it can look like only part of the actor or actress is actually on stage, it does it slowly and in a sideways motion which with some dry ice and the correct lighting could be very effective," Cheryl remarked thoughtfully, staring at the ashtray which was now being levitated in a swishing movement across the table.

"Barty," Tavistock snapped, "stop messing about."

The ashtray was placed carefully back on the table and the beer mats were quickly replaced under each persons drink.

"The thing with the Corsican Trap was that it was built for one specific play called 'The Corsican Brothers', the brothers were twins ..." Tavistock continued, studiously ignoring Barty who was sitting on the edge of the table and staring happily down Cheryl's gaping and amply filled blouse.

"Just like Barty and Ronnie," Lou breathed, his eyes beginning to glitter.

"Exactly, and that can be explained at the time by someone we are going to plant in the audience, a very loud someone." Tavistock smiled at the realisation that Bob would finally have his fifteen minutes of fame and all of them on camera. "And the final crushing piece of evidence which will completely floor our darling Ronald is that Kiki here won't be wearing any shoes."

"No shoes?" Kiki reiterated.

"How on earth will not wearing shoes frighten that bastard into a full confession?" Cheryl asked.

"Because he took them," Tavistock bluntly stated.

"He what?" Kiki barked.

"He likes to take things, he always has," Tavistock answered at a nod from Barty. "And no one but Barty knows that he has the shoes; the police don't, although they may suspect it on the grounds that the corpse was only wearing a suit and socks, but they don't know what happened to them after they were removed."

"He takes trophies," Lou remarked, beginning to understand. "So if he is taken away by the police and they can get a search warrant before he's released from custody thcy might …"

"Find out where he keeps it all, which will be all the proof we need," Cheryl breathed.

"This sounds like you think that he killed more than one person," Kiki whispered, clearly appalled.

"We think that if he has Barty's shoes then he may have other, er, trophies of other killings, but frankly we only have a rough idea, or rather an educated guess about who else may have been, er, pushed towards the ether." Tavistock nodded.

"Do you think that he might … that he might … might have killed my Dad?" Kiki asked, her carmine lips trembling slightly.

"Circumstantial evidence does point that way," Tavistock agreed.

"I only ask because they never found his wedding ring, I checked you see when I was older, because I wanted something, anything really to remember him by, and when I looked at the record of what he'd left behind, his wedding ring was missing; he left it to me, you see, and the solicitor checked with the police records and it wasn't on the body, and he always wore it because mum …" Kiki stumbled over the last word and then took a tremulous breath. Tavistock handed her a paper tissue and Cheryl patted her kindly on the shoulder.

After a loud and defiant blowing of the nose and dabbing at the running mascara dribbling in black blobs down her cheeks, Kiki swallowed and then after silently regarding each of her companions announced. "I'll do it."

"Good, er, girl," Tavistock announced approvingly. "So that's settled then. Kiki, you will dress up as Barty with help from Cheryl and rise up through the stage floor at the given time, I'll denounce him as a fraternal killer and Lou will record it for posterity and the Manx courts."

"And what do I do?" Barty asked.

"Whatever I tell you to do," Mannanan answered, stepping away from the alcove in which he'd been quietly eavesdropping.

Chapter Twelve

Harry and Tony looked up at the wooden floor above their heads and knew that the job they had set themselves was going to be extremely tough if not downright filthy.

"Are you sure it will still work?" Tony asked, rubbing a patch of stubble on his chin that the razor had missed.

"Well, it worked for the centenary celebrations when they exhumed the original script of 'The Corsican Brothers'," Harry remarked.

"Well, it may very well have worked then but that doesn't mean that it will work now." Tony grumbled. Harry stood beside him and scratched the back of his neck in a thoughtful fashion.

"Besides which we don't have any way of having a quick rehearsal to make sure it still works without it actually killing anyone tonight," Tony added, as he stood and regarded the wooden skeleton of the trap with slightly cynical eyes. In the dark it had seemed like the safest, most solid place in the world but now under the glare of several high wattage naked light bulbs, it looked old and tired.

"It will work," Harry firmly stated, patting him on the shoulder.

"But it must be at least a hundred years old!" Tony moaned.

"Well, actually, no it isn't; it's a very good reproduction of the original using all the materials that the original engineers used."

"Really?"

"Don't you be put off by its appearance, lad, young David Wilmore rebuilt it, took him long enough but he got there in the end … well he did eventually. Had a bit of a setback when they first tested it though …"

"Oh … why what happened?"

"… well lad, they realised on the first attempt that the actor's head might have had to be a bit … er … elastic."

"You mean …"

"When they first put it through its paces the test pilot's head was going at a different rate to the rest of the body still concealed under the stage." Harry grinned and made stretching motions with his hands.

Tony gulped and went a paler shade of grey.

"But nobody actually died, so as the Bard himself would say, 'All's well that ends well'."

"Right," Tony cautiously agreed as he regarded the wheels and pulleys with a certain amount of deep-seated suspicion and then gave the beamed frame a hefty push.

"Anyway, the good news is that we do now have the time to get it up and running, as we had a bit of a meeting upstairs and Russell has agreed to close the place down in order for us to ascertain that no one will be decapitated during this evening's performance."

"Oh right, good, I think …"

"Aye up lad, by the pricking of my thumbs something wicked this way comes," Harry chuckled as a solitary figure edged its way cautiously towards them.

"So how does it work?" a woman's voice asked from the dust-laden shadows.

Tony jumped and then upon seeing who it was, smiled warmly.

Jemima stood beside him and gave him a brief hug. "Thought you might like a sandwich or two, in case you felt tempted to pinch someone else's," she chuckled, producing a Clingfilm-wrapped wad of bread from the depths of a plastic carrier bag.

"Sorry, couldn't get any horseradish so I had to resort to mustard instead," she added, handing the package over.

Tony laughed outright and pointed upwards.

"Well if I understand it right, love, what is supposed to happen is that above us is a long narrow hole in the stage like a trench. And covering the trench is what they call a length of scruto …"

"Scruto?"

"It's a sort of wide belt of thin, narrow pieces of wood held together from underneath, by a long piece of jute, which is stretched over the opening and then is wrapped around two drums either side of the trap." Harry nodded in agreement and Tony gave a brief grin before resorting to the notes that Russell had previously given him.

"OK … so that must be that bit there?" Jemima reasoned and pointed to a length of wooden slats, not unlike a section of closed Venetian blind, which hung down at one end of the device.

"That's right," Tony agreed. "Well, as the trap moves, that's that box thing that looks a bit like a cross between an orange box and a stool, it travels up the slope on a sort of rail ..." He moved towards the middle of the wooden frame and inspected the wooden rail before continuing, Jemima following his every move with interest '... and then the actor is seen by the audience as coming slowly up out of the ground but sideways and not straight up. The scruto stops them from seeing the hole or trench behind him, because it travels at the same speed covering the gap where he's been and vanishing from the bit where he's just about to go. All in all I should think it would be very scary seen from the auditorium, especially with a bit of dry ice and the right lighting."

"Hummm." Jemima pulled an earlobe in a thoughtful fashion and regarded the mechanism with a frown. "It looks a bit heavy for just one person to manage."

"Ah, well now ... there we might have a real problem. Three people can apparently manage it but with four it would be a lot easier."

"Then it's just as well that Isla is looking after the children for the first night as I need a night off and have decided to go to the theatre."

"Oh?" Tony enquired, still reading avidly from his notes.

"I mean, I said I was going to support a friend, I just omitted to say which one."

"Thanks love." Tony gave her a long and loving hug until he was interrupted by Harry tapping him on the shoulder with the end of a large fat yellow candle.

"Leave it for the bedroom, lad, we have work to do ensuring this is dust-free and that all working and movable parts are actually working and movable," Harry whispered into his ear.

Some time later they stopped and regarded their

handiwork with approbation.

"I think that's about as much as we can do," Tony affirmed, worrying at a blister on his hand.

"Let's just hope it goes all right on the night then," Harry muttered.

"I ought to get back to the kids and settle them down for Isla; do you want a lift back to the hospital?" Jemima asked, oblivious to Harry's uncharacteristically helpful presence.

"You go on up, love, I'll just stay down here until it's time, after all it will look a bit odd if I'm caught prowling around too often and Bob did say to keep out of sight until Brian nails Mr West."

"Especially as they took the cloak and mask back," Jemima retorted, grinning. Reaching up she planted a kiss directly on his lips and with a smile departed to the upper world.

Tony watched her leave with an equally sickly smile on his face until Harry thumped him hard in the small of the back as Jemima finally disappeared into the gloom and her retreating footsteps could no longer be heard.

"Funnily enough ..." Harry snorted, handing Tony the mask and cloak he had been hiding behind some spare wood. "You might actually need this in about five minutes."

"Why?"

"Management meeting on stage."

"Management meeting?"

"Yes lad, and since I'm now on speaking terms with the rest of the fools on this particular ship, I'm having to finally work, which in turn means that you have to too."

Five minutes later, after Russell had carefully locked all the doors to the outside world and ensured that everyone else had left the theatre building and wasn't expected back until seven o'clock at the earliest, the ghosts, Tony Banks aka 'The Phantom', Bob Callow, Tavistock Allan, Brian Clague, Lou Sphinx, and Cheryl and Kiki West met up under the glare of the working lights.

Mannanan sauntered across the stage and stopped above the Corsican Trap.

"So this is where it lurks, eh?" he enquired tapping the floor with his foot.

"Do you all know what you have to do?" he asked, looking around. Everyone nodded with the exception of the dancers, who bobbed with nervousness.

"In that case, Russell, it's over to you."

Russell Gillings-Cooper regarded his assembled troops with a certain degree of trepidation and cleared his throat.

"Harry, did you get Tony to grease the sled and the rails with tallow as I instructed?"

"Yes I did and I can confirm that all working parts are now working; well they are down there I'm not sure about up here as yet."

Russell smiled briefly before continuing, "I had a word with Richard and told him that we needed to do a few alterations to the stage but that we wouldn't upset the set, so you had better mark where everything is and put the sofa back exactly where it is now." Everyone looked around and then nodded as one.

"OK, now listen very carefully as I will say this only once …" There was a titter from the older listeners whilst the younger members of the team looked blank. Russell gave a small internal sigh and then continued in his usual dry manner. "What we have to do next is very important and I want you all to understand that we have just enough time to do this properly because if we don't and somebody rushes something, Kiki might end up … er … a little stretched."

There were more nods and serious faces, even the dancers stood quietly to attention, feet turned outwards.

"Right then troops, firstly we have to move the furniture back and lift the carpet," Russell barked, moving adroitly away from the centre of the stage.

There was a burst of movement around Russell's stationary form, as the entire set was removed and placed carefully in the wings and at the very back of the stage area. Russell watched, making mental notes of everything that was going on around him. Finally the area was clear and his motley crew turned as one to find out what he wanted them to do next. Russell waited for complete silence and then continued, "Good work team, very good work, and now we can sort out the trap itself. I will now mark out the area of floor we have to remove with chalk and then after it's gone we can connect both ends of the length of scruto, from left to right with the hole through which young Kiki will ascend. The aperture looks a bit like a square of wood with a ring like a loo seat in the middle."

"But won't the audience notice the hole?" Kiki asked.

"No, not really, you see the opening is covered in bristles through which the platform underneath, on which you will be standing, will force you up and through."

Kiki looked if anything less convinced but remained silent.

After Russell was satisfied that everything was correctly prepared and in place, he gathered his team about him and rubbing his hands in a pleased fashion, announced that all was ready for the first test.

Kiki, Tony, Harry and Cheryl disappeared downstairs with Bob, who was the liaison man between Russell and the backroom boys, as he had humorously christened them.

The remaining helpers stood in a group at the front of the stage and watched as the mechanism was started up. Very slowly first a head and then a complete torso was seen to glide across the stage from left to right. At the end Kiki stepped forward and moved across the floor to the front where she peered into the darkened auditorium.

"OK, well that appears to be all right, a bit juddery but with the dry ice not too noticeable. You lot down there reel it back and then do it again, only this time, Kiki, I want you to go back down afterwards," Russell barked, moving a stray prop away with his foot.

Again the lift was tested and again it worked; there was a combined sigh of relief from everyone concerned and then the trap was carefully set at the start position, a length of hardboard was placed over the scruto and the hole and then a carpet was laid over the lot. Finally the entire set was reinstated in as near its original positioning as possible.

Tavistock moved around and then, turning, regarded Russell with a questioning frown.

"So what happens during the seance scene?"

"We have actually thought quite a bit about that, my dear. While the furniture is being hauled about by the actors playing Charles, Ruth, Dr Bradman and Mrs Bradman, Rupert and Cedric will carefully pull away the carpet and Edwin will remove the hardboard with Mannanan's help. The lights are only dimly on above Madame Arcati and to confuse the scene even more we will set dry ice to drift across the stage. Now this is very, very important; when you get to the bit about 'anybody being there' and the business with the knocking, we will ensure that the table you are all seated around really does rise up and fall over, that way all the other members of the onstage cast will be so flabbergasted that they will wait for you. You will then fall into what they think is a real trance and Kiki will rise from the stage."

"At that point Bob will loudly explain that the only time that he saw anyone do what is being done, was during the centenary performance of 'The Corsican Brothers' in which a murdered twin comes back to confront his murderer," Mannanan interjected.

"Then I walk to the front of the stage and point to Ronnie, you wake up and ask if a Ronnie West is in the audience and then we play it by ear," Kiki added, looking rather pleased at finally playing a more decisive role in her older brother's downfall.

"Whilst at the same time I have been filming everything for a broadcast about the theatre ghosts for a Midsummer Eve's special, which is being done live from the studio. At that point I think that my producer will have already had us patched in on a live feed and it should be enough to convince the police, especially if we manage somehow to get Ronnie to confess," Lou grumbled, still not totally convinced that their plan would actually work.

"Oh he'll confess all right, even if I have to swan up there and pull him onto the stage myself," Barty rumbled. "And if he doesn't I shall give him such a fright that he'll expire on the spot," he then added as a happy afterthought.

They all regarded each other in unspoken camaraderie and then silently departed to take up their positions for that evening's first night performance. Behind them the theatre waited in semi-darkness, with a heightened feeling of expectation, for the final light in the stalls to dim and for the drop curtain to rise, ready for the Middling Players and their production of Noel Coward's improbable farce 'Blithe Spirit'.

★ ★ ★

Stella sat and regarded her gently swelling foot with dismay bordering on hysteria, her wig was askew half-on and half-off her bowed head and a large tear wobbled dramatically upon the end of her nose. "You can't possibly go on like that, let alone ride a bike!" Sarah exclaimed, handing her a man-sized paper tissue she had finally managed to extract from the box she habitually kept beside her collection of cosmetics.

"I suppose I'll have to tell Richard," Stella mumbled.

"Of course you will, and the sooner the better in my book," growled Marianna, teasing a curl into position with a ferociously steaming curling tong.

Stella sniffed again, only this time more because of the acrid smell of burning hair rather than for dramatic effect. "Are you sure those things aren't too hot?" she asked.

"Of course not," Marianna scoffed, laying it down and reaching for a base colour.

It was at that point that Richard knocked on the door and after a tersely spat 'Enter,' discovered one of his key actresses in a state of undress and acute discomfort.

"What the hell happened?" he asked, kneeling down to inspect the swelling foot.

"The stupid woman tripped," Marianna grunted.

"I did not trip! I was felled by one of your many items of self-improvement, most of which, may I add, don't appear to be working," Stella retorted. "I've told you time after time that you ought to be more careful where you leave your clutter."

"Oh, give me a break!" Marianna exploded. "It was one very small box of curling tongs and just because you never

ever look where you are going we will have to cancel the play."

"I shall continue," Stella whimpered in a piteous fashion. "After all, the show must go on."

"Well, actually no it can't," Richard stated, his examination of the damaged appendage now completed.

"But ..."

"I'm very sorry, Stella, but there is no way you can hobble on like that, I shall get someone to drive you to Accident and Emergency and then I shall have to have a word with Russell about giving people back their money. As for tomorrow, maybe you can go on with crutches or something." Richard rose and gave Marianna a baleful glare before adding, "And you can clear up your things, I have a teenage daughter with a bedroom actually tidier than this."

Marianna had the grace to blush and began to furtively pack some of her fifty-two items of make-up and hair products into a large plastic case.

Tavistock, who had entered quietly behind her husband, cleared her throat.

"Ahem ... er, I could go on instead, I mean I can't act but I do know the lines."

Everyone stopped and stared at her.

"You do?" Marianna breathed.

"Really?" Richard asked, hope beginning to be glimpsed at the end of the proverbial tunnel.

"What, all of them?" Stella asked, frankly incredulous.

"Well, most of them; I sort of learnt them while I was prompting for you, the times when Ivy couldn't make it, and of course Richard is always quoting."

"I am?"

"Oh yes, incessantly, ask the children, they were all for

having you sectioned at one point," Tavistock uttered with feeling.

"Well …" Richard looked around uncertainly.

"It will be fine," Stella reassured him firmly, "Tavistock can go on instead of me, just for tonight. Maybe you could make an announcement about my fall and her stepping in and if the worst comes to the worst she reads from the script, after all it's not as if it hasn't been done before … besides which the costume is one of those kaftan things … one size fits all and with a few scarves and beads she will at least look like a dotty old psychic."

Richard looked from one anxious face to the other and then at his wife's. "Are you really sure? I mean you've always said you've hated acting and performing in public, that's why you avoid those festival things."

"I don't avoid them, I just don't like them and it's more the time away from you and the children than the actual speaking, besides which it can't be more nerve-wracking than live radio, at least I have a script and I can always ad lib if necessary."

"Talk about delphiniums if all else fails," Stella advised. "Geilgud always did – or was it lupins?"

"Well, I think you're very brave and I and Geoff will help all we can, when we're on stage," Marianna asserted, beaming.

"And you have the prompt, even if …" Sarah's voice tailed off uncertainly.

"She's deaf and is always at least two pages behind the rest of us, except of course when she falls asleep, then panics and prompts us from the next scene," Marianna remarked acidly.

"Well, I admit that she's not perfect …" Richard

muttered.

"Not perfect! Richard, if she were a horse they'd have shot her years ago," Marianna scoffed.

"I was going to add that that is the reason why Tavistock stood in as often as she did, which I suppose is just as well," Richard hastily added.

Tavistock moved to the rack of costumes hanging from a stainless-steel rail at jaunty angles against the wall and fingered a long paisley shawl.

"Well, I suppose I'd better change," she mumbled.

"And I'll do your hair and make-up," Marianna stated, unpacking her plastic case of beauty products.

"I'll leave you to it then," Richard mumbled before helping Stella to hobble from the room.

As they left Tavistock could still hear the previous Madame Arcati complaining bitterly that she was sure that the wretched box had moved as she entered the room and if it wasn't for the fact that there had been nobody there, that someone had shoved her forward from behind.

* * *

Half an hour later Tavistock waited in the wings for her cue, complete with an elderly bicycle which she had to ride through the open French windows. Barty stood behind her with his ghostly copy of the script and earnestly tried to make out the really long words. Mannanan had painstakingly helped him split up the ones with more than one syllable but he was still having a bit of difficulty.

Harry, Tony, Jemima and Cheryl, who was still applying the finishing touches to Kiki's makeup, waited under the stage for Mervin to tell them that the set was clear, whilst various bodies alive and dead hung in the darkened shadows of the wings ready to get the trap working.

Russell sat in his office and regarded his half-full bottle of venerable golden-coloured malt with unbridled desire, knowing full well that the last thing he'd need would be a befuddled head.

Bob Callow watched the audience take their collective seats from the dark comfort of the box next to the one currently occupied by Barty West, his current wife and the minister.

The minister's wife had been sent off to buy a box of Maltesers and was currently knocking back a large gin in the bar.

There was a buzz in the auditorium as the audience gathered and the lights slowly dimmed to reveal the gloriously painted drop curtain and its attendant buxom beauties.

Slowly the curtain rose and the set was revealed in its painted and primped perfection, the audience clapped enthusiastically as was traditional on the unveiling of a satisfactory staging and Ruth entered, closely followed by an anxious-looking maid in an old-fashioned black dress, starched apron and beribboned cap.

Bartholomew West sucked noisily on a barley sugar and hung expectantly over the lip of the box, which he always reserved on any first night that he was personally sponsoring. Tonight he would enjoy the show and tomorrow he would sort out the last remnants of his recently marketed empire and disappear to somewhere warm, foreign and with absolutely no extradition treaty with the UK Government. 'And Frankie says that Zimbabwe is really warm at the moment if not downright hot,' he silently mused as the audience settled down in the seats below him.

His wife tittered at one of the minister's many and

increasingly lame attempts at the concept known as a joke and Bartholomew shivered internally. "I am emphatically not," he thought, "going to take her though," which on balance made the entire project more than usually satisfactory.

Unfortunately the young man he had set up in a diminutive Dockside apartment was too well versed in his affairs to be included in his plans for a luxurious exile, but he was one of many young men and under-age girls that Bartholomew had resorted to over the years and so he had every faith in being able to groom another.

Bartholomew chuckled as the lines gathered momentum and the wit that was still Noel Coward sparkled in the glare of the spotlights illuminating the stage and the bickering forms of Charles and Ruth, his elegant but overbearing second wife.

Chapter Thirteen

"Barty?"

"What?"

"Do you want a choccy?"

Bartholomew West glared at his wife and then resumed his previous posture of attentive listening.

"Well, do you, pet?" his wife whined insistently.

Bartholomew gritted his teeth and willed her to drop down dead.

"Barty?" she prodded him in the spine and simpered ingratiatingly as carefully controlling his temper, he forced the single monosyllable of "No" from between clenched jaws. The minister sitting beside him shuffled uneasily. Bartholomew's wife might once have been a page three girl and even now at the ripe old age of thirty, as she kept announcing with a little girl simper to anyone that would listen, was still extremely attractive in a plastic Barbie doll kind of way. Unfortunately she had the retention span of the average goldfish and made the entire Dingle Clan look like Harvard professors in comparison.

Bartholomew turned and eyed his top heavy wife in her new Prada suit with unmitigated loathing. "Could you just shut up for ten minutes please, sweetheart?"

"Of course I can, sweetums," she cooed and batted her very long, very false eyelashes at him, her newly inflated Botoxed lips pouting girlishly. "Why?" she added, "has it all gone dark, has the play finished, sweetums? Because if it has, it was very short and I think you ought to at least ask for your money back and ..."

"Shut up, shut up, shut up," Bartholomew hissed. "It has gone dark because Madame Arcati has just turned all the lights off so that she can get in the mood for the seance scene, and you are ruining it for everyone; why the hell didn't you stay at home and watch Eastenders like I asked you to?"

"Oh, but ..."

"Shut the fuck up or I will kill you with my bare hands," Bartholomew threatened, "and give me those sweets." Bartholomew threw the chocolates on the floor, gave his now trembling spouse a final hate-filled glance, muttered "Sorry for that interruption, Sir" to the minister and his embarrassed wife and resumed his attentive viewing of the darkened stage. He wasn't sure why all the furniture had mysteriously disappeared, apart from a small table and accompanying chairs, which had been moved to the front, but he was dying to find out. Four darkened figures who were valiantly trying not to listen to what was going on in the box above their heads, as were the rest of the audience, sat on the stage in silence around the small solitary table on light bentwood chairs, one of which stood empty and awaiting the presence of Madame Arcati who was currently flitting about the stage in an odd sort of inane dance whilst waving a hankie around.

"I knew that her brief encounter with those Morris Dancers would someday come in handy," Bob Callow whispered to Lou Sphinx, who was crouched beside him in the box next door to the one occupied by Bartholomew West and his illustrious party. "And now it has," he sniggered.

"Lights!" Madame Arcati shouted. The entire stage went black, the carpet over the Corsican Trap was silently and quickly carried off by ghostly hands and the hardboard covering the hole in the stage was just as silently removed and placed black side up, behind the hulk of the baby grand piano.

A faint light emanated from above the heads of the sitters, much to their concern, as in rehearsals it had been much brighter.

"Oh dear!" Mrs Bradman said, and meant it.

Slowly a faint shimmering mist rolled across the stage from the wings as Madame Arcati resumed her place and her lines.

"Quiet please!" Tavistock ordered, before sitting on the empty seat. Originally she had been supposed to collect a stool from under the piano but had changed the script as Russell had been adamant that the last thing they needed was to draw attention to the hardboard and the newly opened floor.

The audience sat and waited with bated breath; the actors held theirs too, hoping that Tavistock would remember her lines and Richard prayed to any God that might be around that the play wouldn't get any worse.

"Is there anyone there?" Tavistock asked.

A faint ribbon of curling vapour wound itself about the stage and fell slowly over the edge and into the orchestra pit.

"Is there anyone there?" she asked again.

There was a longer pause and a faint rumble from below the stage.

One rap for yes ... two raps for no. Now then, is there anyone there?"

The table shot upwards to the startled disbelief of the surrounding actors and two loud knocks were distinctly heard.

"What the hell was that!" Charles shouted.

"Oh God, look!" Ruth screamed as a head slowly rose from the ground.

"You say there is somebody there who wishes to speak to someone here?"

Ruth, Charles, Dr and Mrs Bradman stared at Madame Arcati and the emerging figure with their mouths open and Richard stood rigidly in the wings and gasped in mounting horror at the rising apparition.

Bartholomew West, who had followed the emergence of the ghostly form with a good deal of interest, suddenly went cold all over; the figure had a definite look about him, a familiar nightmarish clarity, normally only previously achieved at four thirty in the morning after too much whisky and shellfish.

Tavistock wandered slowly over to the grey and faintly gleaming phantasm as it carefully stepped from the now fully raised trap and held out her hands.

"Do you want to speak to somebody here, dear?" she asked.

The figure nodded once in a measured way and the audience now completely mesmerised, sat in fascinated silence and waited. Even the elderly boiled sweet suckers from

Stockport had desisted from their synchronised mastication.

"Could you point that person out, please?" Madame Arcati asked, her voice carrying clearly across the stage and out into the waiting auditorium.

Kiki West turned, and walking in grey socks to the front, the seventies-style suit clinging to her padded frame, paused and then pointed to the box containing the West party.

Bob on cue almost shouted out his scripted words in sheer nervousness.

"I reckon he came up in the Corsican Trap, just like in the play, you know the one where the murdered twin comes back from the dead for justice and revenge."

"Twin?" Bartholomew gulped, and eyed his suddenly visible loquacious neighbour with fearful interest.

"Oh yes, it was his twin, see, as it was the whole point of the play really, mind you the play was crap but the trap was brilliant."

"So that's probably a real man down there?" Bartholomew asked.

"Oh I shouldn't think so, it's been blocked up for years, I mean you'd have a ruddy great hole in the stage if it was working, Health and Safety all over the place with ruddy great manuals and measuring devices, I mean can you imagine what they'd say?" Bob snorted derisively.

The minister nodded in agreement as Bob resumed his seat and Lou focused his camera sights on a gently quaking Bartholomew West.

"Is there a Ronnie West in the auditorium?" Madame Arcati continued as if she hadn't heard Bob's interruption. The audience however continued to stare up at the boxes as one by one they recognised Bartholomew's worn and worried features.

"No there ain't, but there is a Barty West, isn't there, sweetums?" Bartholomew's wife shouted back.

Bartholomew gave her a look of muted horror and looked frantically around for some means of escape, only to discover the massive frame of Lou Sphinx behind him with a camera, a sound man and their respective equipment; Lou gave him a big grin and winked broadly.

"No, I'm sorry, but you must have it wrong. Barty West is here, Ronnie West murdered him and took his shoes, that's why we go barefoot, barefoot that's why we go barefoot ...." Tavistock collapsed and the ghostly figure of Barty West vanished from sight, hidden in part by the mounting wall of mist and the sparsely lit stage.

Richard marched onto the set and strode over to his wife, who now lay in a prone position on the floor.

"Get those bloody lights up now! This instant!" He shouted out.

The stage lights suddenly sprang into action and to the amazement of all, the Corsican Trap was nowhere to be seen and all the stage furniture was back in its original position, including the large ornate Chinese carpet which had covered most of the visible floor.

Someone in the darkened depths of the stalls clapped enthusiastically.

"Must have been one of those mass hysterical jobs when loads of people see the same impossible thing," Bob chuckled, leaning over to the next box and fixing the trapped Ronnie West with a manic and cheesy grin.

"But ... But ..." Bartholomew stammered.

"Why did she think you were Ronnie, love? Ronnie's dead," his wife whispered, uncertainly backing away from him. The audience, their collective attention now firmly fixed on the two boxes, waited; even the minister and his wife were listening with rapt concentration.

"Yes Mr West, our millions of viewers would also like an answer to that rather pertinent question? Why would a spirit return from the other side just to tell us that he was your brother and that we had actually got your name wrong for all these years?" Lou slowly asked the live feed now up and running and the agitated ramblings of his director clearly audible as the device in his left ear made a dash for freedom.

"Mr West, you may be interested to know that we are now live to the nation and I'm sure that the nation is holding its breath over your answer, as we all are, here in this delightful little theatre on the Isle of Man."

"What answer?" Bartholomew aka Ronnie West screamed.

"Who are you? And why would your twin brother accuse you, and in such a public place, of murdering him?"

"My name is Bartholomew West, and …"

"Oh no it isn't, it's Ronnie West, and you hit me over the head with a spade and dumped me in concrete," Barty hissed at him from the rim of the dress circle.

Ronnie, his eyes standing out on stalks, turned back towards the audience and knew that he would now never get to his warm and watery hideaway.

"Hey, haven't I seen you somewhere before?" Lou enquired. "Hey, I remember, you were the man that stuffed that body behind the boiler; I saw you do it. Hey everyone, this is the guy that can break every bone in your body with a baseball bat if you don't fit right."

"You couldn't possibly have seen that, no one was there;

I made sure that no one was there ..." Ronnie screeched, and then losing every vestige of common sense, he grabbed the minister and produced a wicked looking flick-knife from his pocket.

"What the ..." the minister squawked.

"Let me out or I'll cut the fat git's throat," Ronnie shouted dementedly.

"Leave him alone, you murderer!" the minister's wife screamed, and hit him on the side of the head with her handbag, which was large, heavy and shaped very much like a brick.

"Ow!" Ronnie bellowed.

"You unmitigated bastard, don't you dare touch her," the minister roared, and stamped hard on his foot as Ronnie swung the knife towards his wife.

Lou continued filming and watched with sheer delight as a large Alsatian leapt from the side of the dress circle and into the box, which was now feeling very cramped indeed. The dog bit Ronnie very hard on the hand holding the weapon and Ronnie staggered over the side of the box and fell towards the upturned faces of the audience below. He landed on the ample form of an elderly ice-cream seller who promptly hit him on the nose with a small tub of raspberry ripple.

Mike, who had followed his quarry over the edge, growled threateningly at his feet and then moved very slowly until his face was drooling over the upturned visage of a partially stunned Ronald West. He then began to eat the melting ice-cream.

"Ronald West," a voice intoned, "I am arresting you on the suspicion of murdering one Daryl Smith; you do not have to say anything but ..."

Ronnie was helped to a standing position by a variety of hands, some without a pulse, and was then escorted, still muttering in a rambling and shocked fashion, to the patiently waiting police car, which was now parked alongside the steps outside the main entrance with lights flashing and siren wailing.

Barty, Mannanan and the rest of the theatre ghosts watched Ronnie West being manhandled into the car with unbridled delight from the unseen safety of the outside balcony.

The cast of 'Blithe Spirit' sat in their respective dressing rooms and mutely removed their costumes, while the audience, who had had a thoroughly good time, departed for their respective homes in a voluble and satisfied frame of mind.

Ronnie West's wife sat in the now empty booth and shook her hair extensions.

"Is it over?" she asked a passing cleaner, "Only I didn't get it at all. I thought there was a ghost and lots of funny lines?"

The cleaner gave her an odd look and then left at almost a run to fetch the manager; her brushes clutched in both claw-like hands she pattered away towards Russell's office. Russell, who had been in the process of being interviewed by a local hack, who uncharacteristically didn't want Russell to write the piece himself and then send it in, listened politely to her request to sort out the lunatic in the box, as she had to contend with enough nutters at home and so she was buggered if she was going to start dealing with them at work.

Chapter Fourteen

Brian Clague regarded the far wall of the office with a puzzled frown; there was something not quite right about it. Ronnie West's secretary bobbed up and down beside him like a waterlogged plastic duck and clucked despairingly.

"But he doesn't have anything else in here," she whimpered, "apart from his desk, his chair and the plasma screen."

"Well, where does he keep all his files then?" Brian asked, trying desperately hard not to panic.

"In the filing cabinets in my office and you've already looked in there," the little woman beside him sniffed, remembering the resultant mess with a shudder, it was going to take hours to clean it all up and she still hadn't managed to find the time to type up her own CV for the employment agency. At this rate it would be at least an extra day or so before she could quietly leave and after what her loathed boss had been charged with, she and in particular her rather staid and conservative husband weren't exactly overjoyed at still being associated with the West empire in any shape or form. She sighed in a pointed fashion and handed over a bunch of keys, which Ronnie West had once grudgingly given her for emergency use only.

"These are for all the drawers in his desk; you can try in there if you must because frankly I've got more than enough work to do without sorting them out as well," she huffily explained.

It was at that point that Kiki West sailed into the room, gaily enveloped in a miasma of expensive French perfume and trailing behind her slim form, a wealth of brilliantly coloured silk scarves.

Brian stopped in the act of opening the first drawer and glared at her.

"What the hell do you think you're doing here?" he demanded.

"Well, darling boy, I now apparently own this company, or at least I do according to my father's will, which clearly stated 'that in the event of both brothers being either dead, or arrested for any serious crimes such as murder, larceny or fraud, that Kirk West inherit it all, lock, stock and smoking barrel'."

"Oh."

"Which is good news for you, my adorable plod, as I will be able to put the entire weight of the firm behind helping you to successfully convict my disgusting sibling."

"Right, er, thanks," Brian stuttered, opening the other drawer on the left, which held nothing more exciting than three unopened packets of striped men's shirts and several items of plain white underwear, together with a large tin of assorted biscuits and recent copies of both *Hello* and *Playboy* magazines.

"Well, I'm glad to see that my horrible big brother had

every social nicety covered!" Kiki stated, pointing to the glossy covers of both publications. She then smiled sweetly and wandered around the room searching for dust with an effeminately held and rather grimy be-ringed index finger. Eventually she stopped her irritating perambulations and stared at the wall behind Brian's questing frame.

"That's odd," she muttered and walked towards the offending structure, which she began to carefully tap with the flat of her hand.

"What is?" Brian asked in mid-rummage.

"This wall is somehow wrong."

"Oh?"

"Have you ever read any Conan Doyle, Inspector."

"Not recently, no."

"Oh you should, my dear, you really should ... The thing is, if you had, you might have come across the one about the inimitable Sherlock Holmes and the builder of somewhere or other – could have been Finchley or Epsom or, well ... anyway a place just outside central London ..."

Brian continued to stare at her and then stepped back abruptly as the sound made by Kiki banging her hand against the wall suddenly changed, becoming hollow in tone.

"... Anyway in this particular gory tale the builder had a false room made, so that he could hide out; I think Agatha Christie used the same ploy in one of her Poirot yarns, no matter. The point is that my brother, being as devious a little sod as they make 'em, used to read all the old detective stories and I wouldn't be at all surprised if that's what he's had done here, and he would have done it himself, so that no one else would have known, especially little Miss Twin Set and Pearls next door."

The hollow sound continued for a few feet and then abruptly stopped.

"Well, if it is a room it's very small," Kiki remarked. "I wonder how you get at it?"

"Perhaps there's a button or some sort of lever?" Brian mused, carefully feeling the emulsion painted surface for some sort of device. After a fruitless search they both stopped and regarded the blank and bland surface with mutual frustration.

"How clever was this brother of yours?" Brian finally asked scratching his chin.

"Well …" Kiki mused, rubbing the side of her *retroussé* nose with an immaculately manicured nail. "He wasn't so much clever as sly, if you see what I mean."

"Hummm," Brian pondered.

"I mean if he really wanted to hide something he'd probably have put it in the most obvious place he could think of."

"Which would be where?"

"I dunno really, it would have to be in plain sight … how about a switch of some sort? He was lazy as well as devious and he wouldn't have wanted to have to do too much every time he wanted to open it, whatever it is."

Brian looked around the room and then felt his eyes drawn back time and again to the large plasma screen in front of him and directly opposite the possible secret bolthole.

"Why would you need four remote controls for one television?" he asked as he finally realised what had been niggling at his subconscious for some time.

"Four?"

"Yes, there are four in that drawer."

He pointed to the lower right hand area of the desk and Kiki, grinning, removed all of the plastic devices from the cluttered contents.

The first one switched on the TV and they both stared mutely at the sight of a voluptuous and markedly top heavy teenager modelling a very small swimsuit.

"That is just sooo tacky," Kiki remarked, switching it off and trying the second black plastic box.

The late Fred Dibnah appeared and hit a piece of brass pipe with a hammer. "So that must be the satellite one then," Kiki announced and laid it to rest beside the other remote.

The next plastic oblong switched on the DVD player and the fourth one appeared, to begin with, to do absolutely nothing.

There was a slight noise behind them and then part of the wall pivoted silently inwards, revealing a small square space in which sat a long thin cupboard, not unlike a cross between a wardrobe and an old-fashioned tallboy.

Kiki swallowed and carefully placed the remote back down on the desk. Brian stared in fascination and then hurriedly recalled his team, who were all currently searching the rest of the offices and a promenade apartment.

When they had arrived, recording equipment and forensic boffin at the ready, Brian very slowly opened the two doors which were concealing what he hoped would be the final proof of Ronnie West's murderous tendencies.

"If this was one of those American mini-series I bet you a quid that something disgusting is bound to fall out, maybe not even a partial something, maybe a whole someone, a very skinny whole someone?"

"Kiki, shut up."

"Yes Sir."

Brian stepped back and allowed the spectacled scene of crime technicians to peruse the contents.

"Well?" Kiki asked, nervously fiddling with a pendulous earring.

"There are a pair of men's leather shoes in there, together with a small plain gold signet ring and a baby's rattle."

"A rattle?" Kiki whispered in barely concealed revulsion.

"Why the hell would he have a rattle in there? I mean, I presume that's what it is, some sort of trophy room?"

"I believe so, yes," Brian agreed, settling his tired bulk down on the floor, with his back to the large window with its panoramic view of Onchan Head and miles of white flecked waves.

"Anything else?" Kiki asked, sitting down beside him with a silky rustle.

"Small cardboard boxes carefully labelled in a numeric code, or at least it looks like code. I have no idea of the exact contents but if they are all trophies of some sort or another your brother was a very, very, busy boy and probably quite mad."

"Oh, I don't think he was mad," Kiki mused. "Just totally self-obsessed and utterly selfish."

"Right."

"I think that he knew exactly what he was doing, he just didn't care; he never has, and as for morals I doubt very much if he ever had any."

"So you personally believe that he was and still is completely sane?"

"Totally."

"Well that gives me a lot to start with, that and the shoes."

"I'm glad, you know, that you found them. I liked Barty, he was always kind to me, let me stay up to watch TV, bought me old *Marvel* comics and outfits for my Barbie dolls … he even made a few of them."

"Do you still miss him then?"

"Oh yes I do … quite a lot of the time actually. I mean … don't get me wrong, I can live without him, I've had to, but if I'm totally honest with myself I sometimes wonder just what our lives would have been like if Dad had fought back and pushed Ronnie under that bus."

Kiki and Brian slowly stood up and stared beyond the polished pane of glass and upwards into a cloud-swept sky in a companionable silence, broken by the happy sounds of an investigative team with a clear and undisputed result. Outside a gull soared across the ragged cliffs below them and vanished behind a wave-flecked wall, only to return and wheeling, chase another out of sight.

* * *

Barty West stood in the newly converted cellar and regarded the chrome and glass lights with interest.

"Nice," he remarked, "I've never seen square glass light bulbs before."

"Very smart," Mannanan agreed, plumping up one of the mock-suede cushions.

"I suppose you've brought me down for a reason," Barty muttered, playing with a framed print of two people dancing on the sand, whilst a bored and wet butler holding a large and recalcitrant black umbrella looked on.

"That maid looks really hacked off," Barty mused, tracing a line of thunderous cloud with his finger.

"Probably wants to dance with her own lover not watch somebody else's."

"Or she could be in love with the boss and …" Barty

stopped and turned abruptly. “Why am I here, guv?”

“Because this is where you died and this is where you can now pass on, justice has been done and your brother has finally confessed, although only on television and before he was arrested by the police.”

“He never said he was sorry though, the murderous fat bastard.”

“To be honest I don’t think he was.”

“Charming.”

“He didn’t appear to be sorry about anything, except being found out and even then he seems to have taken it in his stride.”

“Why did he do it?”

“Who knows? Perhaps he was upset that you stopped him setting fire to the theatre. Perhaps his nose had been put out of joint because you wouldn’t do what he wanted and you squealed to the police. Or perhaps he just enjoyed killing people. The only thing we and the police know for certain is that he’s refusing to say anything at all.”

“No remorse, not even a shrug?”

“Not an iota.”

“So this is it then.”

“I’m afraid so.”

“Wot if, wot if …

“Yes, what?”

“I don’t want to go.”

“Why on earth would you do that? You can’t possibly want to spend the rest of your life in a bar?”

“Why not? I mean have you seen that bird wot works here at the weekends, cor, she’s well tasty.”

“Tasty.”

“Stacked, you know …”

"Yes … I believe that I unfortunately do … stacked … not a bad simile, that."

"Er …. Right I fink … anyway I don't really want to move on. Couldn't I stay?"

"And do what?"

"I could assist you …"

"Me?"

"I could feed the cat, do all the legwork, interview offending entities, learn how to read proper. You know, the big words, the ones made up of other ones all strung together, so's that people think you're dead clever instead of just being dead."

"Well …"

"I could learn how to fill in all that paper work … like that pile you got given this morning and hid in the waste-paper bin."

"You saw that?"

"Wasn't difficult to miss, there was tons of it, although why it was wet is a bit of a mystery like …."

"Ah well, that was probably because I tried to flush it first."

"Ahh, wot about trying the odd match and some of that lighter fuel you keep in your desk?"

"I did, unfortunately after the last lot of forms the department sent in to me, this lot appeared to be extremely flame resistant."

"Ah, the wonders of modern science."

"Tell me about it … I still have problems with the combustion engine and don't even get me started on those dreadful flying toilet rolls."

"Oh … wot … you mean planes."

"I said don't even get me started … good grief what in

heaven's name is that?" Mannanan moved towards the bar area and regarded a stuffed and mounted plastic fish with interest.

"What on earth would anyone want to hang that on a wall for? It doesn't even look real; I mean look at the size of its head for one thing?" Mannanan grumbled.

"You walk past it and it sings," Barty advised with a grin.

"Sings?"

"And waggles its tail, it's quite funny the first time."

"And this is progress?"

"Oh yes, this is most definitely progress." Barty smiled and blew on the offending vertebrate, which promptly started up a tinny rendition of 'Born in the USA'. Mannanan watched and then abruptly turned on his heel and began to mount the stairs to the ground floor two at a time. At the top he paused and called back down, "Well if you're coming, you'd better get a move on, I want all those forms completed by Thursday and then we have to go see a monk about a dog down at Rushen Abbey."

"A dog?"

"Apparently he, the monk that is not the dog, likes dropping twigs on its head at around midnight after he leaves the Whitestone pub and the neighbours have complained."

"About the pub?"

"No, about the dog … and the singing doesn't help."

"Singing?"

"Gregorian chants."

"Ah, well now, I can see why they'd have words about that sort of fing, antisocial that is, chanting and such, now if he'd regaled them with a bit of Elvis or Morrissey I bet yer a tenner that no one would have batted the proverbial eyebrow."

Barty grinned up at his new boss and Mannanan, shaking his head, vanished in a flurry of Hugo Boss aftershave, closely followed by his beaming assistant.

Behind them a shaft of light fell amid the newly polished low tables and 'Bushy Brew' beer mats, featuring an inebriated fox and a semi-clad Stone Age sex pot wearing not much more than a knotted hanky and a utility belt.

"Look, Mr West, are you coming or what? Only I have to be in Peel by lunchtime," a disembodied voice querulously demanded of the empty room.

⋆ ⋆ ⋆

Richard Allan surveyed his cast and his motley collection of stagehands with a certain amount of not entirely sober pride, and wobbled.

"I'd just like to thay ..."

"Speech," a young lad at the back demanded, drumming on the coffee table in front of him with his feet.

"Er ... well now ... er ... I'd just like to thay thank you, to all of the ... all the cast and especially to our dear Stella, who like the trooper she is, acted her socks off this evening and last night despite her crutches ..."

"And the Zimmer frame, that got a lot of laughs," Stella's daughter wheezed as a large scotch and ginger went down the wrong way.

"A stroke of genius, Stella, by the way..." Richard grinned and accepted the large drink with matching umbrella that Doris the props pressed into his hand; it was bright blue in colour and fizzed but he sipped it anyway and wobbled a bit more.

"Only because some idiot pinched her crutches," Marianna shouted as she tried to nibble the earlobe of a young man she'd picked up the previous night at the Hilton.

"Right, right, anyway thanks everyone and again …"

"Richard!" Tavistock bellowed from the bar. "Shut up and bring on the buffet – I'm starving!" There was raucous applause and good natured clapping, as Richard muttered "I'm coming, my darling, my little piranha fish …" into the mike in front of him, which had decided to finally work and therefore picked up every single mimicked note.

Tavistock, who was trying to tempt Bob Callow into trying a cocktail named 'Between the Sheets', turned and glared at her advancing spouse.

"That was actually funny," she growled, scowling. "And since when did you do humour?" she added, flicking a peanut at him.

"I'll have a Screwdriver," Bob advised the barmaid.

"A Screwdriver?" His wife Moira queried, glancing down at the lengthy list of cocktails.

"Oh yes, definitely, a Screwdriver is in order; the plumber phoned while you were out at the shops and says he can turn up next week so I'll be seeing quite a lot of them over the forthcoming weeks," Bob grunted morosely. "And possibly months …" he added as a bitter afterthought, remembering one particular plumber, aptly called 'Leaky' by other members of the building fraternity, whose inept ministrations had ended with six inches of water in the kitchen when he was supposed to be putting in a new bathroom suite and several yards of piping which had turned into a sprinkler system almost overnight

In a concealed alcove Lou Sphinx got down on one knee and proposed to Cheryl, who had discarded her baggy cardigan in favour of a miniscule skirt of red sequins and a black PVC corset. Cheryl stared mutely down at him and then promptly pulled him onto her lap, and cooing delightedly, accepted the large diamond and sapphire ring from the proffered satin-lined box with alacrity.

Kiki, watching from a safe distance, grinned and turned back to converse with her elderly secretary about the rival merits of Botox and silicone implants.

Brian and Caro, minus their most recent infant, ploughed through the sea of celebrating thespians and their attendant acolytes until they finally managed to spot Bob Callow at the bar, deep in conversation with a young man carrying a large selection of tapas on a tray.

"Try the marinated squid rings," Caro urged, helping herself to a small ceramic pot.

"Actually I rather fancied the chorizo and pine nuts," Bob grunted.

"Bob?"

"Yes Brian."

"What did you say to Lou Sphinx? Not that it now has any bearing on the case at all since Ronnie has made a full and fairly frank confession and the theatre are not demanding anything …"

"Nothing," Bob replied, picking up a large piece of sausage with a wooden cocktail stick.

"Nothing!" Tavistock and Brian exclaimed in unison.

"Nothing," Lou Sphinx affirmed from behind them.

"A bottle of your finest bubbles and some glasses, one for each of these good people … actually make that two bottles; I'm feeling generous," Lou bellowed though the tumult. A lanky barman with acne and a ring through his eyebrow nodded and tottered off to the fridge.

"Champagne?" Brian queried as Cheryl staggered towards them on six-inch gold heels.

"This darling woman has just agreed to make me the happiest of men, haven't you my love?" Lou cooed, cuddling her ample frame.

"Hang on a minute, I thought that you two couldn't stand the sight of each other?" Tavistock murmured, pouncing on the last dish of anchovy-stuffed olives.

"All for show, sweetie, all for show, just like letting everyone think that Bob here had had a bit of a barney with me, when in actual fact the flatfooted plonker had fallen over a case of Newcastle Brown I was attempting to stow away just as he pushed his way into my dressing room."

"But we heard you arguing with someone. You were at it hammer and tongs," Brian grunted, taking a bite out of a filo-wrapped prawn.

"Arguing?" Lou muttered, struggling to recall that particular moment. "Oh, I know what that was … you must have heard me playing one of the interviews I'd recorded for your local radio station."

"Must have been something like that because there was nobody else there, at least no one you could actually see," Bob muttered, giving Lou a quietly suspicious glance.

"Bob?" Tavistock demanded, regarding him with a steely sparkle in her eyes. "Is any of this true?"

"Well, about the beer and falling flat on my face … yes, the thing was that Lou asked me really nicely if I'd keep it a secret, as he wanted everyone to think that he was being threatened and had no friends."

"Which was a bit of a lie but Cheryl and I had been working on getting revenge off that thug Ronnie for years."

"Why?" Brian asked, dipping a battered chicken goujon into a lime-and-lemon sauce.

"He raped Cheryl's younger sister at some party," Lou

advised them. Everyone at the bar stopped eating and stared as one, first at Cheryl and then back at Lou who was blithely continuing, "The bastard apparently dropped that date rape stuff in her drink and forced her into doing certain acts which he taped and then sent her a copy of to stop her going to the police." Brian swallowed and patted Lou sympathetically on the shoulder.

"It was her hen night, you see," Cheryl explained, a bitter note edging into her usually happy voice.

"She cancelled the wedding at the last minute and discovered she was pregnant a month later, drank half a bottle of vodka and jumped off a bridge," Lou rumbled.

"Baby's rattle," Brian whispered to himself.

"What?" Bob asked, catching the end word.

"Nothing, nothing at all, just like your phantom row, er, just as a matter of interest how did you persuade Bob not to say anything?"

"Ah well, there you have me, how indeed?" Lou chuckled, pouring out the champagne into various flutes and passing them around.

"Let's just put it this way, when the new firm gets launched and the office is finally open we won't be short of a beer or two," Bob laughed, sipping on the golden bubbles.

"Anyway, on the understanding that all's well that ends well, I propose a toast," Richard barked, finally joining them after his inebriated perambulation of the room.

"A toast!" Tavistock shouted above the hubbub and raised her glass.

"To the Corsican Trap." Richard yelled.

"The Corsican Trap," they all replied, and drank.

Above them a gibbous moon moved slowly across the sky trailing long spindles of vaporous clouds in its wake, whilst the Gaiety Theatre sat and waited patiently for the next opening night.

Linda Mann worked in the offshore finance sector for ten years until settling on the Isle of Man where she is now married with three children. She was a member of the Isle of Man Arts Council and Chairman of the Film and Literature Panel for four years but she now concentrates on writing, including skits for the satirical news programme 'The Headlines Again' on Manx Radio. She has written four supernatural crime novels – Mist, The Tidemaster, Mr Boots and The Corsican Trap – available or forthcoming from Priory Press.